There was a dog standing in the middle of the road watching her. It was black, high and thin, with a sharp pointed nose and prick ears, and as it moved its head slightly the moonlight caught its eyes and they were bright green, like emeralds. Lucy made a noise in her throat between a scream and a gasp. She slid off the gate and began to run back down the lane, and as she did so she had a second's glimpse of antlers, raised above the hedge, moving, dark and forked against the sky....

The WILD HUNT HUNT OF THE GHOST HOUNDS

PENELOPE LIVELY

ACE FANTASY BOOKS
NEW YORK

This Ace Fantasy Book
contains the complete text
of the original edition. It has
been completely reset in a
typeface designed for easy reading,
and was printed from new film.

THE WILD HUNT OF THE GHOST HOUNDS

An Ace Fantasy Book / published by arrangement with
the author

PRINTING HISTORY
William Heinemann Ltd. edition published 1971
Puffin Books edition published 1984
Ace Fantasy edition / April 1986

ISBN: 0-441-88810-0

Ace Fantasy Books are published by The Berkley Publishing Group,
200 Madison Avenue, New York, New York 10016.
PRINTED IN THE UNITED STATES OF AMERICA

To Jack

AUTHOR'S NOTE

"Let no one be surprised at what we are about to relate, for it was general knowledge throughout the whole country that...many men both saw and heard a great number of huntsmen hunting. The huntsmen were black, huge and hideous, and rode on black he-goats, and their hounds were jet black, with eyes like saucers, and horrible."
—*Anglo-Saxon Chronicle*, trans. G. N. Garmonsway (Dent, 1953)

"The Yeff Hounds, or Ghost Pack, were heard pattering through Stogumber after midnight this year, but no one looked out to see them, even nowadays. They are known to run through the village and down towards Roebuck, then on up to Wills Neck."
—Member of Stogumber Women's Institute, 1960 in R. L. Tongue, *Somerset Folklore*, ed. K. Briggs (The Folklore Society, County Folklore Vol. VIII, 1965)

≡ ONE ≡

THE TRAIN HAD stopped in a cutting, so steep that Lucy, staring through the window, could see the grassy slopes beyond captured in intense detail only a yard or two away: flowers, insects, patches of vivid red earth. She became intimate with this miniature landscape, alone with it in a sudden silence, and then the train jolted, oozed steam from somewhere beneath, and moved on between shoulders of Somerset hillside. She settled herself back in the seat and looked round the empty compartment. After the crowded urgency of the London train, with swaying bodies packed tight against one another, this train was an unhurried haven, almost empty. A handful of people had got on at Taunton— schoolchildren and women with shopping baskets—but Lucy had remained alone in her compartment: through the partition came the comfortable rise and fall of women's voices. The seats were squashy, their cut velvet covers worn right down and faded where the sun had fallen on them. The dust that Lucy had dislodged when she sat down still hung, spinning, in a shaft of sunlight. There were arm-rests to be pulled down, a table that could be raised by the window,

and pictures above the seats, two at each side. They were
enlarged photographs, yellowing a little with age—Porlock
Bay and Dunkery Beacon behind her, and, in front, fishing
boats in Watchet harbour on one side and on the other a
stag, his antlered head rearing magnificently against the
background of Exmoor.

She could still remember the names of the stations in the
chain between Taunton and Minehead. They were magical,
infinitely familiar—Norton Fitzwarren, Bishop's Lydeard,
Crowcombe, Stogumber, Williton, Watchet, Washford, Blue
Anchor, Dunster . . . She began to wonder who would meet
her. Just her aunt? Or would the others be there too? She
was enjoying this solitary journey, mulling over her memories and nursing anticipation like an unopened present so
that arrival, she feared, might almost be an anticlimax. It
would not be long now: they had left the flat, chequered
fields of Taunton Vale some time ago and were winding
deep into the hills. Lucy sat, staring out of the window,
savouring every moment, searching for remembered landmarks. From time to time the moving fields, trees, lanes,
would resolve themselves for an instant into a picture that
seemed familiar—a cottage crouching against a steep bank,
with grazing sheep in profile on the slope behind, or a distant
line of hills spread against the sky. It was strange to make
this journey alone. Last time she had been seven, bouncing
from seat to seat, eating sandwiches and chocolate, com-
plaining that the journey would never end. Her mother had
sat there, in the seat by the window . . . Lucy took an apple
out of her pocket and began to eat it savagely. Light blinked
on and off as the train plunged through short tunnels, and
then slowed down abruptly as a station platform loomed
ahead among the fields.

Stogumber. How had she ever thought this journey long?

Already it was half over. Three people got off the train and a porter unloaded a crate and some parcels from the guard's van. From a cottage garden two small children were waving and all along the platform bright flowers glowed in neat beds. All of a sudden Lucy felt a rush of excitement—it would be good to see Aunt Mabel, and wonderful to be at Hagworthy again. It should be a good summer. Aunt Mabel had explained, in her abrupt but kindly way, why she hadn't invited her for so long. She was busy with her own affairs, she led a quiet life, and she couldn't be doing with unattended small children. "But now that she is twelve," she had written, "or is it twelve? Anyway, no matter—now that she's older, I assume she is a sensible body and can amuse herself. She will remember the place, and not expect too much excitement, and other children seem to mess about quite happily in the school holidays. Send her down as soon as you like." She hadn't said anything about Kester, or Caroline and Louise.

"Will they still be there?" said Lucy anxiously.

"How should I know?" her father had said. "Presumably. I shouldn't think things change much in Hagworthy." He was obviously relieved by the invitation. The holidays were always a problem, with him working all day and Lucy alone and bored.

"What does Aunt Mabel do all the time?" To a seven-year-old Lucy she had been a hazy figure, benign but remote, busy with fork and trowel in the cottage garden, or stumping off into the fields.

"She's a botanist. And she's got her garden. She's perfectly happy."

"Doesn't she get lonely?"

"No. That's how she likes to be. She's a very self-contained person. Always was, even when we were children." Aunt Mabel was his older sister. "Do you think you'll be all right? She'll expect you to look after yourself, you know."

"Oh, yes," said Lucy. "At least if it's like it was. It was always lovely at Hagworthy."

A bank covered with primroses . . . Rolling down it, laughing . . . she and Caroline, or was it Louise? And a stream, running beside a lane somewhere, all dark and mossy. They'd made a dam, and an island, she and Kester, for hours and hours, sprawled face down above the water. She used to be taller than Kester, just a bit—perhaps it would be the other way round now. And there'd been a time on a beach, when they'd all gone on a picnic, and Kester got his shorts wet and Caroline's mother made him put on a pair of the girls'—it must have been at Blue Anchor.

The train had stood a long time at Stogumber. Lucy shifted restlessly and stared at the picture of the stag in front of her. The guard, standing on the platform just outside the window, was reflected in the glass so that for a moment the stag seemed to have a man's face below the antlers, staring at her without expression in the silent, empty compartment. The sun had gone in and a few drops of rain spattered against the glass as she looked away again and up to the cottages spilling down the hillside above the platform. The train shook, and began to move.

Only two more stops. She checked her luggage in the rack, and felt in her pocket for the ticket. The present for Aunt Mabel was in her suitcase. They had bought it yesterday, in one of the big West End bookshops, a beautifully illustrated flower-book.

"I hope she hasn't got it," said Lucy.

"I hope she didn't write it," said her father, and they'd looked at the jacket again quickly, and laughed.

"Might she have?"

"Oh yes, she's quite an expert, old Mabel."

The train lumbered on. Fields tipped away steeply downwards, or rose sharply away from the track and hung above the train so that red cows stared curiously down into the compartment. Sometimes a gap would open up between the steep slopes and show a wider world of distant blue hills hung with slaty clouds, and then abruptly close again as the train plunged down into another cutting, choked with cascading grass that almost brushed the windows.

They stopped at Williton, and then moved on in a wide loop towards the coast to take in Watchet before doubling back inland. Lucy pulled down the window to look out at the flat grey sea. The Bristol Channel. It didn't look very appetizing. She seemed to remember running with Kester on golden sands—or perhaps that was somewhere else, a confusion of memories.

I do hope he's come to the station with Aunt Mabel. I s'pose I'll feel a bit shy at first. Probably he will too. And the others.

In Watchet harbour the tide was out. Rowing boats slopped in the mud.

Now they were winding away from the sea, back inland again. Lucy's stomach was lurching a little, and there was a familiar creep of sickness. Mustn't get all worked up. She got her cases down, stood them on the seat, and looked at herself in the mirror. A pale, pointed face peered back, scowling a little, thin fair hair hanging straight at either side. She practised a confident smile, combed her hair, and dealt with a smudge of dirt on her cheek. A bit better. The smile wouldn't last, she knew that—Lucy's natural gloom, her father called it—but the rest might. There was a stain on her shirt, and her skirt was deeply creased in ridges across the front: for a moment she saw herself as the others would see her, stepping off the train, and was dismayed.

Don't be ridiculous—they won't care. We were always scruffy at Hagworthy—gumboots and jeans, and that. Aunt Mabel's the sort of person who doesn't care tuppence what people look like.

Kester'll wear long trousers, like the boys at school. He's thirteen now. Funny.

The train had begun the long run inland, through hills rising steeply to little, wooded peaks and past huddles of ochre-coloured cottages. It was raining, a fine, misting rain that streaked the windows and drifted in veils across the grass, rising as much as falling. Aunt Mabel, she remembered, ignored weather. If you were going for a walk you went for it, rain or no rain. Much of the time at Hagworthy seemed to have been spent splashing enjoyably through puddles, with the rain all warm and wet on your face . . . And those deep, deep lanes, with the greenery arching up either side and almost meeting overhead, so that you seemed to walk in a tunnel. Hadn't there been a place somewhere where they used to jump from one side to the other, right over the lane? Or, at least, Caroline and Kester had, and she had fallen and hurt her knee, and there'd been a business trailing back to get it plastered up.

Engrossed in thought, she failed to notice that the train was slowing up again until suddenly the end of the platform slid into view alongside and the guard was shouting the name of the station. She assembled her luggage again and stood between the seats, swaying from side to side, waiting for the train to stop.

Stepping out on to the platform, she looked round expectantly. Two other people got off the train, but apart from the porter there was no one else to be seen. She picked up the suitcases and began to walk towards the ticket office with a sudden sinking feeling. Surely her father hadn't made a muddle over the day? And then a remembered figure appeared at the flight of steps leading up from the little car park below the station—Aunt Mabel, in the same hairy suit that she had said goodbye in five years ago, peering round short-sightedly, heaving a little as she got her breath back after the climb.

They kissed, awkwardly. The porter took Lucy's cases, and produced a crate of bottles and a parcel. Could Miss Clough kindly drop them off at Hagworthy?

The crate and the suitcases quite filled the back seat of Aunt Mabel's small car. Lucy got into the front seat: obviously there would have been no room for Kester and the girls. No doubt that was why they hadn't come. She glanced sideways at Aunt Mabel, who was hunting for the car keys in a handbag that was a turmoil of gloves, handkerchiefs, and pieces of paper. She seemed quite undisturbed by its loss, and she had said none of the conventional things about how Lucy had grown, had she had a good journey, and how was her father. She had simply absorbed her niece, along with the crate and the parcel.

Presently the key was found, on the floor, and they set off.

"I don't imagine you remember the way," said Aunt Mabel, changing gear noisily as they rounded the corner on to the main road.

"You turn left at the crossroads into a very narrow lane where it's difficult to pass things, and then it's all twisty and up and down for about four miles until the village. There's one bit where you can see the beginning of Exmoor, and your cottage is on the right past the post office and the smith, before you get to the pub."

"Good gracious! I didn't think small children noticed so much. What were you—seven?"

Lucy nodded. They had turned into the lane now, and Aunt Mabel was driving in short bursts, in order, as she explained, to dodge from one passing-place to another, with the minimum time in between.

"The worst thing to meet is the milk-lorry. Quite dreadful—you may have to back half a mile. Caravans are another nightmare."

Lucy laughed. The hedges were almost meeting above the car. Meadowsweet foamed on either side, the smell drifting through the windows. "I thought Kester might be at the station."

Aunt Mabel seemed not to hear. She had slowed up to negotiate a tractor. Lucy had to say it again.

"Kester? Oh, Mrs. Lang's lad. You remember him, do you? Yes, he'd be about your age, I suppose."

There was a pause.

"Does he know I'm going to be here for the holidays?"

"Oh, I daresay," said Aunt Mabel vaguely. "Things get around in Hagworthy. He's a bright boy, I'm told. Goes to the Grammar School now."

Lucy frowned: the smell of the meadowsweet was sickly, really quite overpowering.

They had reached the top of the hill. Aunt Mabel slowed up at the top as though the car, like her, needed to recover itself after a climb. Fields and hedges sloped up and down in front of them, all curves and angles, splashed with the dark shapes of trees and the pink streaks of lanes. On the horizon, hills rose to the sky, dun-coloured, tinged with blue, on a more majestic scale.

Aunt Mabel said, "The Brendons. Remember? And the moor over that way. I daresay you went up there. You can't see the combe yet."

Lucy nodded, staring at the massive sky above the hill. Huge clouds made dramatic shapes, forming and re-forming. A gust of cool air came through the window, and she began to feel better again.

They descended steeply into the valley.

"Hear from your mother much?" said Aunt Mabel abruptly.

"Yes. She's living in South America. They've got a baby. It's called Michael or something."

"Your father managing all right?"

"We've got a Mrs. Taylor. She has to go at four because she's got her own family, but she leaves something and Dad and I cook it."

There was a screech of brakes. A car appeared, coming up the hill. Aunt Mabel leaned back dramatically, braking all over, and the two cars stopped, bonnet to bonnet. She folded her arms and stared malevolently. "Trippers! I'm not backing for them."

There was a brief battle of wills, won by Aunt Mabel. The other car began a slow descent, down a quarter of a mile of twisting lane.

At the bottom they turned right. They were in the valley now, following the road along the bottom, with fields and woods rising steeply at either side, and a stream rushing to the left of the road. It was dark, the light squeezed upwards by the trees, the pink stone walls glittering with moss, the branches overhead ink-black against the sky. Lucy sat bolt upright, staring anxiously ahead. She swung her head round sharply as two girls scrambled over a gate beside the road, and then looked away in disappointment.

"Have Caroline and Louise started their holidays yet?"

Aunt Mabel turned to look at her in perplexity, taking her eyes right off the road.

"Aunt Mabel! There's a man on a bike!"

"Bless me, so there is! Just missed him! Caroline and Louise? Oh, the Norton-Smith girls. No idea, I'm afraid. One sees them often enough. Their backsides glued to a couple of ponies usually. You don't like riding, do you?"

"No," said Lucy. She shrugged herself down into her

coat. It was really quite chilly, and rain was slashing the car windows. The valley was so dark, more like twilight than early afternoon. The car tyres hissed on the wet road.

Suddenly they were in the village. Cottages, their walls stained deeply pink by the Somerset earth, lined the narrow road, jumbled together, seeming to grow out of the hillsides, their gardens rising steeply behind and melting into the fields. The stream, unseen, ran behind a wall. To one side of the road the floor of the valley flattened out for a few hundred yards into meadows and the recreation ground behind the village hall before the ground rose again, up and up, through fields and woods to the distant line of the moor. Lucy shifted about in her seat, trying to take it all in. It seemed smaller, closer together. There was a new shop, and the post office had been painted a different colour. Beyond the cottages, she could just see where the road forked and began to climb up into the hills, swallowed by the dark tongues of woodland that licked up the valley.

"Straight on to the moor," said Aunt Mabel. "Right takes you over the hill to Sweetwater. You'll have to borrow my bike if you want to get about."

Lucy nodded. They were passing the forge. A fire glowed inside, and there was a sound of hammering. A man stood in the doorway, watching the car. Lucy felt his eyes on her and looked away in embarrassment.

They rounded a slight bend and pulled up outside the cottage. "There!" said Aunt Mabel. "Remember it?"

"It's shrunk."

"No, it hasn't. You've grown. You're half a size bigger. Therefore the cottage seems half a size smaller!"

It was cob, with a slate roof, set back from the road in a garden that seemed to overflow. Roses struggled with honeysuckle: white and mauve flowers flowed over the stone walls; hollyhocks rose almost to the eaves.

Lucy helped carry cases and parcels from the car and up the paved path to the front door, wet plants brushing against her legs. Aunt Mabel led the way into the little hall.

It was dark, and smelt of fresh damp earth and flowers, as though the garden were trying to burst in here too. The first objects that caught her eyes were the antlers. There were four pairs, one on each wall, great spliced thing spreading almost to the ceiling, ridged and grooved, but smooth to the touch. She ran her hand over one, feeling the sharp tips.

"Have you always had them? It's funny, I don't remember them. How did you get them? Did you hunt the stags?"

"Good gracious, no. They were given to me, at one time and another. People pick them up, you know, on the moor, when the stags are shedding them. Come and see your room."

The bedrooms had low ceilings, beams, and creaking floors. Lucy's was at the back, looking straight out at the steep hillside, where pink-fleeced sheep grazed on a parallel with the window and the thick grass poured down the slope in a river that was halted only by the wall at the end of the garden. She had to look upwards to see the sky; grey clouds swept right down to the top of the hill.

"Is this the one I had before? I can't remember."

"Probably. Come down when you're ready. I have to feed the chickens, and then we might have some tea."

Left to herself, Lucy unpacked her things, stowed the suitcases under the bed, and explored the room minutely. There was little that was familiar, except a yellowing photograph in a frame, of her father as a small boy and Aunt Mabel, a stout schoolgirl, glowering ferociously from under a pudding-basin hat. Everything in the room was elderly, from the faded cotton bedcover to the lace runner on the dressing-table, excepting only the table-lamp by the bed, which still had the price-ticket on it.

She bought that specially, Lucy thought, and suddenly felt like crying.

There was a bookcase under the window. She went through it carefully. A Bible, Shakespeare, other poetry books, Jane Austen, a few Dickens, Harrison Ainsworth, E. Nesbit in early editions, some flower books, some very old Penguins—yellow and blotched as though they had been read in the rain—a whole series by someone called Charlotte M. Yonge, with pictures of medieval-looking people and gothic castles, *Twenty Years on Exmoor* by "A Somerset Man," and a further assortment of odds and ends. A good hoard for rainy days, anyway. Of which, by the look of things, there were going to be plenty.

Aunt Mabel's room, glimpsed through the open door, was businesslike and unfeminine. The brushes on the dressing-table would have done as well for a dog, and there were no pots and bottles. The bathroom smelt of carbolic, and the towels had a faint tinge of ochre to them, as though the all-pervading earth had got in here too.

Lucy began to go down the stairs, pausing to examine the pictures on the way. There was a water-colour still-life of tulips in a vase, a sepia print of Dunkery Beacon, reminiscent of the photograph in the train, some flower prints, and a large, gloomy etching in a heavy gilt frame. The picture was so dark that she had to stare at it for a minute before she could make any sense of it. It was a moorland scene: dogs and horses crossed a rugged hillside at full gallop. The leading horse was in the act of rising to clear a low bank, and both horse and rider seemed to have stag's antlers attached to their heads. The hounds were odd, too: they had something coming from their mouths, like tongues of flame. Under the picture there was a little gold plaque, and engraved on it in slanting script "The Wild Hunt, by Edward Tiller R.A. 1883."

For some reason the picture chilled her. She hurried past it and went to find Aunt Mabel.

They ate tea in the kitchen, in a companionable silence. Aunt Mabel's dog, a shaggy white thing like an old bathmat, lay in front of the stove, quite immobile except for an occasional convulsive twitch.

"We are enjoying middle age together, he and I," said Aunt Mabel. "Have another scone."

After tea it rained, a steady downpour that streamed off the windows and ran from the gutters, crushing the plants in the garden and filling the air until it felt as though the whole cottage were under water, in a dank, sub-aqueous world. Lucy, who had wanted to go out, sat on the window-seat in the sitting-room and read back numbers of *Punch*, looking out every few minutes. It grew darker and darker.

Aunt Mabel sat at her desk, writing and occasionally referring to a book from the pile beside her. She was, she had explained, preparing a paper for the Botanical Society on the rare grasses of Exmoor.

Just once, she put her pen down and looked across at Lucy. "My dear, I do hope you will find enough to occupy you here. It's a quiet place, you know."

"I like things quiet," said Lucy. "Anyway, there's the others. Kester, and Caroline and Louise."

"Oh. Oh, yes—the children you used to play with. But remember you have all moved on five years. You may have moved in different directions."

Lucy stared. "Oh, I see," she said politely, and returned to her book. Aunt Mabel picked up her pen again. Outside the rain fell in an impenetrable wall, isolating the cottage.

Tomorrow, Lucy thought, it must be fine. Tomorrow she was sure to see them.

≡ TWO ≡

IT WAS SUNNY the next morning. They ate breakfast looking out on to a sparkling garden. Aunt Mabel was more talkative and the dog had recovered consciousness, ambling up and down the garden path and growling dutifully every time someone passed the gate. He was called Whitby, it appeared.

"Why?" said Lucy.

"Do you know, I have quite forgotten. One has these odd impulses. Presumably it had significance at the time."

After breakfast Lucy hung around in the kitchen, while Aunt Mabel went through her post and looked at the newspaper. She wrote her name idly in the dust on the dresser, and then jumped with guilt: she didn't want to imply criticism of the housekeeping. But clearly Aunt Mabel was impervious to dust.

"I have to go up to the woods this morning. I've heard there's some tree-felling going on and I want to check that the orchids are not affected. Would you like to come?"

"Would you mind if I didn't? I thought I'd go and find Caroline and Louise."

She had been watching the gate for the last hour, half-expecting them to appear.

Aunt Mabel did not mind: indeed, she seemed faintly relieved.

The Norton-Smiths' house stood a little way out of the village, further up the valley beyond the cottages, though, again, distance had diminished: it was much nearer than Lucy remembered. She enjoyed the walk, with the sun warm on her back and the hedgerows either side alive with flowers and insects. She turned into the drive and made her way up to the house between neat box hedges, remembering some game they had played jumping over them. At the front door she was seized with nervousness, and had to fight it back before she could ring the bell.

Inside, a voice called, "All right, Mrs. Webb, I'll go."

The woman who opened the door was carelessly, even shabbily, dressed. A crucial button was missing from her blouse, her skirt was faded and pinned where the zip had broken. This seemed to indicate self-confidence rather than poverty, and matched the appearance of the furnishings visible behind her: battered, but originally expensive. She shared with the house, the garden, the stables beyond, an appearance of needing to make no unnecessary statements about a position in the world.

For a moment she stared at Lucy blankly, then recognition broke over her large, sunburned face and she exclaimed, "Why, it's Lucy Clough! How you have grown! The girls will be frightfully thrilled. Caroline! Louise! I bumped into your aunt the other day and she said you were coming down for the hols. What splendid fun!"

Mrs. Norton-Smith towed Lucy into the hall, shouting "Caroline! Come and see who's here!" Lucy had forgotten what a very penetrating voice she had. Indeed, she didn't really remember her. Like Aunt Mabel she had been a shadowy figure, unlikely as this now seemed. It was the girls who had been important.

A woman put her head round the kitchen door and said, "I think they're down in the stables."

"Oh, goodness, yes. They'll be grooming for the gymkhana. Busy day for us, Lucy, there's a do over at Withycombe. I say, would you like to go down and find them. You remember the way?"

Lucy hesitated. Mrs. Norton-Smith brayed with sudden laughter. "Oh, I say, you're not shy, are you? Come on, I'll take you there."

They walked down a short drive, Mrs. Norton-Smith talking loudly and shooting sudden questions to which Lucy mumbled inaudible replies.

There were two ponies in the stable yard. Caroline, two feet taller and very plump, was doing something to one of them with a brush. Louise, equally unrecognizable, was pushing heaps of manure around with a broom. Mrs. Norton-Smith said she must go back to the house and get on, and she'd leave them to it.

"It's awfully nice to see you again, Lucy," said Caroline. "Are you going to be here all the holidays?"

"Yes."

"Oh, jolly good. I say, d'you mind if we get on with doing the ponies? We've got a gymkhana this afternoon. Do stay and talk to us."

Lucy sat on a mounting-block. The ponies swished, blew and stamped. "Where do you go to school?" said Louise.

"It's a comprehensive. Near where we live in London."

"Oh," said Caroline blankly. "Is it nice?"

"Yes. At least I like it."

"We go to a boarding-school in Kent. Cranford Towers.

It's where Mummy went. I say, Louise, you must do something about Fetter's tail. It looks ghastly."

"I s'pose it's difficult to get any riding in London," said Louise, with concern. "We might be able to let you have a go. The trouble is the ponies are a bit highly-strung."

"It doesn't matter," said Lucy. "I don't think I want to." The others looked surprised.

"Do you still go to that place where there's a waterfall?" said Lucy, picking at a piece of moss with her finger-nail. "We had a picnic there once."

"Oh, I remember. And Louise fell in the stream!" They all laughed.

"Kester was there too. I haven't seen him yet."

"Kester Lang? Oh, we don't see him much now."

"Why not?"

"Oh, well, we wouldn't really, would we?" said Caroline vaguely. "Let's have the curry-comb a minute, Louise."

Mrs. Norton-Smith appeared round the corner of the house and shouted that there was squash and biscuits if they'd like some. They trooped into the kitchen, Caroline and Louise shedding drifts of straw and horse-hair.

"Awfully sorry we can't take you with us to the gymkhana, Lucy."

Mrs. Norton-Smith was cramming a basket with sandwiches and thermoses. "Trouble is we're a bit of a tight squeeze already, one way and another."

Caroline said, "Would you like to come along to the smithy with us? We've got to get Timber shod before we go."

"Now?"

"Yes."

"All right. I mean, I'd like to."

"Bet you were glad to get away from London for the

summer," said Mrs. Norton-Smith. "Ghastly place for children. You'll have a super time at Hagworthy. The girls always find it's one mad rush in the summer—one thing after another. We're going to have a rather special fête this year—in another month or so. To raise money for the church roof, you know—the poor old thing's about to collapse. Luckily we've got this new vicar. Frightfully nice man—full of ideas."

"We'd better go, Mummy. The smith takes ages sometimes."

"All right. I suppose you'd better have a wash."

Caroline and Louise vanished upstairs. When they were alone Mrs. Norton-Smith said, "I say, I was frightfully sorry to hear about your parents, Lucy. Jolly bad luck for you. Still, it's all past history now, I daresay. I hear your mother's married again."

"Yes."

"And you've got a little half-brother. Gorgeous. Is he awfully sweet?"

"I don't know, I'm afraid. I've never seen it."

"Oh. Well, I must get on with these sandwiches before the ravening hordes descend."

The girls came back. They collected the ponies from the stables and set off for the village, Caroline and Louise riding and Lucy following a few paces behind. Presently Caroline got off the pony and joined her, leading it.

"It's a shame you don't ride, Lucy."

From the corner of the Norton-Smiths' drive there was a view down the hill to the village. Hagworthy was at the bottom of a steep valley, following the line of the stream, the houses and cottages tumbled together in a heap as though a hand had flung them carelessly down the hillside and they had come to rest together at the bottom. The hills swelled on either side, the diamond-shapes of the fields criss-crossed with dark hedges, the cornfields bright as butter, the occasional patch of bare earth a brilliant pink. Behind, the dark neck of the combe reached up into the line of the hills. Beyond that again was the wild stretch of Exmoor.

"You are lucky," said Lucy, "being here all the time."

"Oh, I *know*. Whoa there, Timber."

They clattered down the village street.

"Here we are," said Caroline.

The smithy was in a shed set back from the road, joined on to a cottage. There was a cobbled yard in front of it and the stream ran over a lane leading off behind, so that you could either wade through it or cross on a little footbridge. Lucy looked round with interest.

"It's a frightfully old place," said Louise. "Mummy says there's always been a forge here, ever since anyone can remember. Always the same family, too. Mr. Hancock's an awfully interesting person; sometimes he's a bit odd, though."

They crossed the cobbles and peered into the darkness of the forge. Someone was hammering inside.

"Mr. Hancock," said Caroline in a loud voice that had become suddenly like her mother's. "It's us. Shall I bring the pony in? Mummy said she'd ring up first so you'd know we were coming."

"Bring her in then."

Lucy, her eyes becoming used to the darker light of the forge, saw the smith bending over the furnace at the back, pumping the bellows. He was a big man, with thick-muscled arms, his face ridged and grooved into deep wrinkles, framed by ears like cups, red and veined in the firelight. He turned for a moment and looked, not at the pony or at Caroline, but at Lucy, with an intent gaze that made her uncomfortable. It was the same man who had watched the car pass yesterday afternoon. Then he turned back to the fire and used the bellows on it, so that flames leaped and a glow rose through the room, lighting up the iron horseshoes ranged on the walls, the tools, anvil, hammers, heaps of nails. He moved across and took the pony's bridle from Caroline, hitching it to a ring on the wall. Whistling through his teeth, he lifted its hind leg, and set it between his knees, his back to the horse. The girls stood at the entrance. Caroline sat down on a block of wood. Once or twice the smith looked up from his work, and each time his eyes fell on Lucy.

"Oh," said Caroline, "this is Lucy Clough. Miss Clough's niece."

"I know that."

There was a movement at the back of the forge. Someone had come through a door leading into the cottage, and was standing behind the furnace. A slight figure, hands thrust in pockets, dark hair, rather long, licked across a pale forehead. A thin face: dark eyes staring.

"Oh," said Caroline, "it's Kester. Weren't you asking about him earlier, Lucy? Of course, Mr. Hancock's his uncle, I'd forgotten. Hello, Kester."

Lucy began an anxious smile.

"This is Lucy, Kester. You remember she used to come down, years ago." Very much in Mrs. Norton-Smith's voice.

Kester took a step forward, looked at Lucy, and nodded without interest. Then he turned to Caroline.

"Hello. Mummy all right, and the ponies?"

Caroline went pink and looked away. "Yes, thank you."

"This is your busy time, of course, isn't it? Right in the horse season, aren't we? Do any good at Dunster?"

"That'll do, boy," said the smith sharply.

"Sorry, Uncle Tom, no offence meant." He looked at Lucy again and said, "They got you all kitted out for the summer? Pony, and all the gear?"

"I can't ride," said Lucy in a strangled voice, and turned her back on him to stare out on to the road.

"Good for you."

"Honestly!" said Louise in a whisper, "he is awful." Lucy took a step inside the forge, carefully not looking at Kester.

The smith had finished taking the old shoe off the pony and was standing by the bench. He was muttering to himself, and seemed angry. Lucy flushed as argument flowered between the man and the boy. "Very full of yourself, aren't you, my lad? If that's the kind of thing you're learning at the Grammar you're best without it, I'd say."

"Oh, for goodness' sake. They're not bothered. It's water off a duck's back."

"I'm not talking about the girls. You know that. It's you. Going on too much. King of the castle. You know what I think."

"I know, Uncle Tom, I know. I should be down there with the bellows, learning the business. Not stood here making remarks."

The smith bent over the forge, scowling, turning the shoe in the flame till it began to glow dully. Kester leaned against the wall, whistling. Once his eyes met Lucy's and he grinned. Caroline and Louise had gone out into the yard pointedly and were sitting, stiff-backed, on a mounting-block.

The smith was handling the hot shoe with pincers. He held it against the hoof and smoke foamed up. The horse shifted, munching the bit, and there was a soft hiss and an acrid smell. Above the noise Lucy heard the man speak again to Kester.

"When I were your age I were out and about with t'other lads in the village, not idling around all day on my own. It's not natural."

Kester said sulkily, "I'm all right. Leave me alone, Uncle. I don't have to go with them all the time if I don't want to, do I?"

"It's that school. Putting daft ideas into your head. I've no patience with it."

"Oh, please, Uncle."

The man grunted. Kester's face was strained, set in obstinate lines. Lucy looked away in embarrassment.

"I heard you scrapping with young Thacker last night," said the smith. "Seems you're set to cause trouble."

"Me! He started it. Anyway we weren't serious."

The man slapped the horse's rump to move it over, and lifted the other hoof. Suddenly he looked straight across at Kester, with a fierce intensity. "Go on the way you are, and we'll have hunting here this summer." Tension hung in the air, like the stillness before a storm.

Caroline had come into the forge. "Oh, Mr. Hancock," she said, "you don't hunt in the summer."

Man and boy turned to look at her, startled out of their involvement with each other. "Maybe we're not talking about the same thing," said the smith sourly. Caroline looked puzzled, then shrugged her shoulders and stood in the doorway, chewing the end of her plait and humming to herself.

Kester leaned against the wall at the back of the forge, chinking something in his pockets, whistling through his teeth. Everything about him suggested defiant confidence, except his eyes, dark and restless, and the mouth, nervously tense, twitching at the corners. The minutes ticked by, the silence broken only by the clatter of the pony's hooves shifting on the stone floor, and the smith's heavy breathing as he worked. And then suddenly Kester swung round and moved towards the door at the back. "I'm off. Cheerio, Uncle."

Lucy said with difficulty, "Goodbye, Kester."

The boy looked at her with faint surprise, "Oh, 'bye."

The smith stood back and slapped the pony's hindquarters. "She'll do. You can take her now." Kester had gone.

On the way out of the yard Caroline said, "Wasn't Kester rude? Honestly, I was so embarrassed."

There were dark clouds massed above the hills, and already warm drops of rain fell. "It's going to rain for your thing," said Lucy. "Why aren't you friends with Kester any more?"

"Oh, well, I mean, it's not like when we were younger, is it? I mean, we aren't interested in the same kind of things, are we? Actually Mummy says he was awfully sweet when he was a little boy but now he's at the Grammar School he's a bit too clever by half. Mrs. Webb says there's an awful fuss with his family because he doesn't want to work in the smithy with his uncle, like they always have done in that family. Actually Mummy says you can't really blame him for that—I mean, boys like that can really get jolly good jobs nowadays if they've got O levels and A levels and things."

Lucy said, "How can you be too clever by half? What's too clever?"

"Oh, well, I mean, brainy people aren't always the nicest people, are they?"

Louise giggled. "That must make us awfully nice!"

"Well, Mummy says she doesn't mind a bit about us being rather dim about work and not passing exams. She says it's much more important to have fun and enjoy things. Riding and everything."

"Are you good at school things, Lucy?"

They were passing Aunt Mabel's garden wall now. Lucy stopped and said abruptly, "I think I'll go in. 'Bye."

"Oh, do you want to? You could come and watch us finish grooming. And we haven't mucked out yet. We don't have to go till after lunch."

"No, thanks."

"Oh. 'Bye then, Lucy. We'll probably see you tomorrow."

Lucy spent the afternoon in the garden with her aunt, removing dead heads from roses.

"We'll promote you to weeding when you've learnt the difference between a plant and a weed," said Aunt Mabel cheerfully. "Did you find those girls this morning, by the way?"

"Yes."

"Have fun?"

"Quite."

There was a silence. After a few minutes Lucy said, "We went to the forge. The smith seemed to know who I was."

"Ah, Mr. Hancock. Yes, I daresay he would—new arrivals seldom go unnoticed. An odd man—but then smiths often are. It's usually a hereditary job, with all sorts of funny superstitions attached to it."

"What superstitions?"

"Oh, this and that. Insights not permitted to the rest of us. Magical powers, even. It's a very old belief, going back to prehistoric times. Wayland Smith, you know, and that sort of thing."

"Oh. When's the hunting season, Aunt Mabel?"

"Autumn through to spring. Why do you ask?"

"Oh, nothing."

In the late afternoon, the rain which had been threatening since midday descended again, and with it a high wind that whipped the trees into a frenzy and sent long ripples across the grass on the hillside.

"This is going to do for my roses," said Aunt Mabel. "Not that it's anything unusual. July's often the worst month."

They went around the cottage closing windows, battening down for the night, as an early dusk closed in. Lucy drew the curtain in her bedroom and squatted down in front of the bookshelf. She had rearranged the books in order of desirability, along with the half-dozen she had brought down with her, library books and two saved-up birthday presents. The most enticing ones she was leaving till last, for a spell of prolonged bad weather, or illness. One should always plan, be prepared for the worst. For this evening, she had selected a Charlotte Yonge—*The Dove in the Eagle's Nest*.

On the way downstairs she found herself deliberately avoiding the picture. Then, at the bottom, she forced herself to go back and look at it. There was no escaping the fact: it had an evil presence.

After supper she mentioned it.

"Oh, that thing on the stairs. Victorian art at its worst, I'm afraid."

"I don't like it."

"Neither do I, particularly. I came across it in a junk shop in Dunster and bought it for the associations."

"The associations?"

"Oh, there's a legend about the Wild Hunt, you know. They're supposed to ride through the village—black dogs and an antlered rider. It's a universal myth, of course—you find it all over Western Europe, but localized in particular places. It comes originally from Scandinavian mythology— Odin is the huntsman. And then, as so often happens, the god has become debased in folklore to the devil. Anyway, the Hunt is associated with Hagworthy, so I thought it appropriate to have the picture. I quite agree with you, though, it's a shocking piece of art."

"That's not why I don't like it," said Lucy, but her aunt had already gone back to her work.

The wind blew harder in the night. Lucy lay awake for a long time listening to it battering against the cottage, clawing at the windows and reaching up under the eaves till the roof creaked and shook. It seemed to be trapped in the cleft between the hillside and the back of the cottage, raging back and forth and Lucy, falling at last into a fitful sleep, heard it still in her dreams and imagined it as a host of restless beings pounding through the air above the combe.

THREE

THE DAYS BEGAN to assume a pattern. By the end of the week Lucy felt as though she had been in Hagworthy for a month or two. When the weather was bad she stayed in the cottage, reading, staring out of the window, or talking to Aunt Mabel. When it was fine she explored the combe. An easy, undemanding relationship had grown up between aunt and niece. They were on the whole much the same kind of person—self-contained, independent, often uncommunicative. Neither wished to interfere with the other.

The village, too, after a little initial curiosity, seemed to have digested Lucy and she could now walk through the narrow lanes between the cottages without faces watching her as she passed. Only Mr. Hancock, she fancied, still fixed her with a speculative look. She learned people's names, and who lived where, and what time the Minehead bus stopped outside the post office, and when the bread van came. Each day had small landmarks—meals, the post, the paper delivery, errands to be done at the shop. Occasionally she walked in the fields and lanes with Aunt Mabel. But time hung a little heavy.

After a few days she returned to the Norton-Smiths. She had seen them riding past the cottage several times, and on one occasion they had stopped and asked her to come up for tea, but she had refused, and later regretted it.

She had seen Kester once, cycling past with another boy, shouting something to him over his shoulder. He had not seen her, or had failed to acknowledge her.

It was a still, hot day, and she could feel the tarmac of the road burning through her thin sandals as she turned into the Norton-Smiths' drive, although it was already late afternoon, almost evening, and the trees on the far side of the fields were trailing long shadows across the grass. Swallows looped above her head, dipping in sudden, close swerves so that she could see the white of their bellies in vivid close-up. As the house came into view she was disconcerted to find a group of people seated in a half-circle under a big chestnut tree. She hesitated, and was about to retreat when Caroline came running across the grass.

"Don't go away, Lucy. It's just Mummy's Committee— the Fête Committee, you know. They're having it outside because Mummy didn't want to stuff indoors on such a lovely evening."

They lay on their stomachs on the grass, snapping the heads off daisies, Caroline and Louise chattering. The voices of the group under the tree drifted across, clear in the evening air. Lucy turned her head sideways to look at them.

They had the faintly uncomfortable look of a group of people come together for a purpose rather than the pleasure of each other's company. There were four women in flowered cotton dresses, several men whom Lucy judged from their appearance to be farmers, sitting restive in deck chairs, as though this idleness irritated them. Cigarette smoke hung blue above their heads. The Vicar sat beside Mrs. Norton-Smith, who alone seemed quite at her ease, leaning back in her chair, knees spread wide apart under a faded cotton skirt with a dropping hem. Her voice rang over the grass, punctuated by occasional murmurs from the others. Only the Vicar seemed able from time to time to stem the flow. Lucy glanced sideways through the grass stems at Caroline and Louise, wondering if their mother embarrassed them.

I'd die if she was my mother, she thought. All noisy and bossy like that.

But the girls' faces were serene, untroubled. "The Fête'll be awful fun," said Caroline. "Will you still be here, Lucy? We usually do the pony rides. She could help us, couldn't she, Lou?"

"What else is there?" said Lucy.

"Oh, the usual things. Tombolas and coconut shies and bran-tubs. And a band and a fancy dress competition and Scout and Guide Parades. Ssh—I want to hear what Mummy's saying."

The Vicar was nodding vigorously as Mrs. Norton-Smith talked. He had a pipe in his mouth which gave him an air of thoughtfulness, of wisdom even, which somehow did not match his face or his way of agreeing enthusiastically with all that was said. "You know, I've been thinking," said Mrs. Norton-Smith, concluding a long speech about the hiring of marquees, "since we are trying to make a special fund-raising effort this year for the Restoration Fund it seems a pity not to make the Fête a bit more of a show. Something out of the ordinary. Try to attract the tourists."

There was a murmur of agreement. One of the women said, "They did a sort of pageant at Porlock the year before last—all in costume and everything, and it was a tremendous draw. They got hundreds of people."

"Super," said Mrs. Norton-Smith enthusiastically. "Anyone know anything about pageants?"

The Vicar had been fidgeting anxiously, trying to find a

gap in the discussion. "Well, I do actually have a scheme I've been keeping up my sleeve. Rather an exciting idea, I feel. I wonder if I might put it to the committee?"

"Jolly good. Go ahead, Vicar."

The Vicar cleared his throat. "Well, it was precisely the tourist trade I had in mind when I thought up my little scheme. I do believe there's a lot of interest in things of local character—like the Cornish floral dances, you know, and that kind of thing—and I thought if we could produce something peculiar to Hagworthy, and advertise it, you know, it might be quite a draw."

"Oh, Vicar," said Mrs. Norton-Smith, "we had the schoolchildren doing a Maypole dance last year and they all got tangled up. It was a frightful disaster."

"Well, no, that wasn't quite what I had in mind. Something rather more ambitious. Indeed, a revival of a traditional custom which I believe to have been quite forgotten." The Vicar beamed round with a kind of triumphant excitement. The women smiled back with polite interest, but there was a stillness among the men.

"I came across it quite by chance really. In one of the parish account books. I've been trying to get some sort of order into the records—sorting out the early volumes, you know—awfully interesting they are too from a historical point of view. I often find myself stopping to read bits; and, to cut a long story short, I noticed this entry, 'To new stockings for the Horn Dancers, 12 pairs at one shilling and sixpence each—18 shillings.' This was in about 1803 or so. So of course I was rather intrigued and I started to look back, and I found other references to Horn Dancers, going back into the eighteenth century. But nothing later than the early nineteenth. Not a single reference."

Mrs. Norton-Smith and the other women were looking puzzled. But one of the men, an elderly farmer, his corduroy trousers still tucked into gumboots, had taken his pipe from his mouth and was staring intently at the Vicar. The girls, fascinated, had stopped talking and edged closer to the group under the tree.

"I don't know if you've ever heard of the Horn Dance of Abbot's Bromley? Well, I fancy there must have been something similar done here, no doubt a very ancient survival. Most interesting. I was quite excited, I can tell you, and even more so when I found this in a cupboard in the vestry that no one had turned out for years."

He dived suddenly behind his chair and pulled something out from under his raincoat, brandishing it triumphantly in front of him.

It was a pair of antlers, mounted on a short thick stick. Below the antlers was a leather mask, with sockets cut for the eyes. The Vicar held it up to his face, with an embarrassed laugh. The antlers reared from his head: behind the mask his eyes glowed, the face quite hidden. Lucy gave a startled gasp, and the farmer leaned forward, his face rigid with alarm.

"Good gracious!" said Mrs. Norton-Smith.

The Vicar put the antlers down again and sat back in his chair, looking round complacently: "Quite a find, wasn't it? So naturally I thought—now why not revive it? The Horn Dance of Hagworthy. We'll check on all the details, and how it was done, and so forth, and I do believe it could be the most tremendous attraction. Tell me, Mr. Taylor, you're a local man born and bred—have you ever heard of the Dance?"

The farmer said, in a clipped voice, "I might have." He clamped his pipe between his teeth and stared at the ground. The Vicar looked put out.

"I think it's an absolutely marvellous idea," said Mrs. Norton-Smith. "You are clever, Vicar. Yes, the more I think about it . . . We can have such fun getting it all organized. And the young people can be the Dancers, of course. How many of them, did you say?"

"Twelve. I'm sorry you're not keen on the idea, Mr. Taylor. I didn't quite gather if you'd heard of it or not?"

There was a pause, then the man said grudgingly, "Perhaps it were done, but not for a hundred year or more." The other men nodded agreement.

"That's just what I thought. But do tell us, why was it abandoned?"

"I don't rightly know," said the farmer. "Maybe it were forgot. I don't like the idea, Vicar; I don't reckon folk would care about that stuff nowadays."

One of the other men said suddenly, "I heard they had to stop it because it were too rough. There were a drowning. And it brought the hunting back. Since the Dance were stopped they don't ride in the combe no more."

Mrs. Norton-Smith looked bewildered. "I beg your pardon?" said the Vicar, but before anyone could say anything else Mrs. Norton-Smith was talking again.

". . . Really such an original idea—an absolute brainwave, Vicar. Do they all have to have these antlers and mask things? It's going to be a bit of a job getting hold of eleven more pairs. We've got one, and there's Mr. Franklin."

"Colonel Ridley at Dunster has quite a few antlers," said one of the other women.

"Jolly good. Oh, we should be able to rake up enough. What do they wear on their bodies?"

"I'm not very clear about that," said the Vicar. "I thought some kind of medieval get-up, perhaps."

The discussion became general and enthusiastic, except for the older men, who sat silent. Once the farmer said again, "I don't like the idea. There'll be folk in the village won't like it."

"Oh, come, Mr. Taylor," said Mrs. Norton-Smith gaily, "don't be stuffy. It'll be the most tremendous fun. The younger people will love it. We shall have a lot of competition to be the Dancers, I'm sure."

"'Twouldn't surely do no harm, George," said one of the other men. "Not nowadays."

"That's the stuff. Now, what do we do about the music?"

Caroline, who had been silently listening with Lucy, said suddenly, "Come on, let's go in and do something. I'm getting midge-bitten." They got up and began to walk away towards the house. Lucy turned once to look back: the nine people under the tree were deep in discussion. The Vicar had driven the stick on which the antlers were mounted into the grass beside his chair: the blank face of the leather mask stared across the lawn towards her and behind it a long, forked shadow streamed out across the grass.

Lucy told her aunt.

"Well, well. How extraordinary. I hardly know this new Vicar, I must say, though after this I shall look at him with renewed interest. One can't help wondering if the man really knows what he's about, but still . . ."

"Caroline and Louise want to be in it," said Lucy. "I think they'll look daft, capering about in fancy dress like that. Do you think tourists will really come?"

"Undoubtedly. So far as that is concerned I should think the Vicar is certainly on the right track."

"They need antlers. Are you going to lend them yours?"

"By all means, if anyone asks for them."

Later, sitting on the garden wall, Lucy reflected. They're mad, she thought, daft, dotty . . . For some obscure reason the idea of the Dance repelled her.

"Didn't the Vicar look funny?" Caroline had said, "with that thing on his head. Honestly, I nearly died."

But Lucy had not found the sight funny. It had haunted her in the night. She had been particularly careful to avoid the picture on her way up to bed.

She shifted a little to avoid a stone that was digging into her back, and propped the book against her knees. This tumbledown bit of the wall was her favourite place to sit and read in the sun. It commanded a view over the lane she could just sit and watch — watch the sunlight race across the fields opposite, and the dome-shapes of the trees echoed in the shapes of the restless clouds above, and the distant white flecks of sheep and the red glow of cattle, and the occasional passer-by in the lane.

There was the scrape of shoes coming from the village, and the whisper of bicycle tyres. That was the trouble with cycling here; you spent as much time pushing as riding. She peered round the wall to see who it was.

Kester. Alone. Pushing his bike up the hill. He hadn't seen her.

She thought: if he takes no notice of me again then that's that. I won't try any more.

She waited till he was almost alongside, and then said abruptly, "Hello."

He looked up, startled. She was almost on a level with his head, a few feet above the sunken lane.

"Oh, hello there." He stopped, leaning on the bike, getting his breath back. Lucy, in a flurry of anxiety, accidentally loosened her grip on the book and it slithered down the wall and landed at Kester's feet.

He stooped to pick it up, looking at the cover. "Oh, that. It's good, isn't it? I got it from the library. Have you read his other ones?"

Lucy nodded, speechless.

Kester looked at her curiously. "You know, I remember

you. Years ago. Up there." He waved in the direction of the Norton-Smiths' house.

"I remembered you, too. I thought about it all the way down here in the train—seeing it all again. And you and Caroline and Louise. And somehow it's all different. Like a different lot of people altogether." She went pink, feeling she had said too much.

"What do you mean?"

Lucy said, "Somehow I can't talk to them any more. We're talking about different things. Not just *what* we talk about, but the way we say it."

"Like they weren't hearing you properly?"

"Yes. Yes, something like that."

"Do you mind?"

"Not really. At least I did at first. Now I'd sooner be by myself."

"You can't always be by yourself. You've got to talk to people, haven't you?"

"Yes. Oh, yes."

They stared at each other: the sun burned Lucy's head. Kester, she saw, had very small freckles each side of his nose, like brown dust.

He said, "You getting on all right? I like your aunt. She'll talk to you in a nice way—interested, but not asking a lot of questions. Do you know what I mean?"

Lucy nodded.

"I can't stand people going on at me. You ought to do this, and why don't you do that. There's a lot of that here, with everybody knowing everybody else. I don't like the holidays any more. It's not so bad in term, when I'm over at the Grammar all day, and just home on the bus in the evening."

"Do you like it? School, I mean."

"It's not so bad. You've got to work hard, mind. Sometimes they don't understand that. Uncle Tom, for instance. My mum's all right about that, though. But I can't talk to her like when I was younger, somehow." He scuffed his foot on the road, frowning.

Lucy said, "I know. You want to but you can't."

There was the sound of hooves clattering down the hill. "Watch it," said Kester, "here comes the cavalry."

Mrs. Norton-Smith appeared round the corner, leading a large brown horse, followed by girls and ponies. When she reached the wall she stopped.

"Hello there, Lucy. Not buried in a book on a nice day like this! You should be up and doing, my dear. We're just taking the mare up on the hill for some fresh grazing."

Louise said, "We're going to Taunton this afternoon to see about the costumes for the Dance. I say, could Lucy come with us, Mummy?"

"Can't see why not. Would you like to, Lucy?"

Lucy said wildly, "I've got to do something with Aunt Mabel."

"Oh, too bad." Mrs. Norton-Smith, who had completely ignored Kester until now, suddenly turned to him as though struck by a thought: "I expect you'll be wanting to take part in the Dance, Kester, won't you? Trouble is we're not going to be able to find room for everyone who wants to so you'd better hurry up and get your name down on the Vicar's list if you want to have a chance. We're going to have a trial run on Saturday evening."

Kester shrank back into the hedge, his face dark and surly, and muttered something inaudible.

"What's that? My dear boy, I can't hear a word you're saying."

"I said I'm not bothered."

Mrs. Norton-Smith said severely, "No, thank you" might

be a nicer way to put it. Really, I thought the schools were supposed to be so good nowadays, but obviously manners aren't top of the list."

"You're just about the only person who doesn't want to, then," said Caroline. "Most people are absolutely dying to. I do think you're silly."

"Never mind, Caroline. Nobody has to. If Kester wants to be left out that's entirely up to him. Come along, girls, we really must be getting on. Goodbye, Lucy."

When they had gone Kester stood in silence, his face red and angry. And then all of a sudden he laughed.

"That lot! They make me want to throw up, they really do. Do you know, if those girls aren't careful they'll turn into those Greek things—half horse and half person. Mummy would be surprised . . . I wonder where she'd keep them? In the stables or the house?"

"Oh, in the house," said Lucy. "She'd be rather pleased, I should think. She'd have to have straw on the beds instead of sheets, and she wouldn't need to bother with cooking any more. She could just put them out to graze on the lawn."

"She'd have to do bowls of bran mash on the Aga."

They both began to laugh hysterically. Kester fell about the lane, clutching his sides.

"She'd plait their tails . . ."

"And put ribbons on them."

"Listen," said Kester suddenly sobering up, "I'm going to Blue Anchor this afternoon to look for fossils. I'm doing a sort of project on geology for school next term. D'you want to come?"

"Me?" said Lucy, glowing. "Honestly? Can I really?"

"Yes, if you want to."

"How do we get there?"

"Bus. Meet you outside the post office at two."

* * *

Waiting at the bus stop, he barely acknowledged her, leaning over the wall and chucking stones into the stream, while Lucy stood disconsolate in the bus shelter, wondering if she had been disowned. But later, sitting together in the back seat of the bus, he explained. "I don't want any trouble with the other boys, see."

"Oh, because I'm a girl."

"That's right. Not that I care that much, really. But they're always getting at me."

The bus wound along the narrow lanes, brushing the hedges on either side, plunging into green tunnels. Lucy, staring out of the window, had the feeling that the countryside was drowning in growth, leaves pouring from the trees and hedges, gradually choking lanes and ditches, the grass and corn spreading in wild profusion, the meadowsweet bubbling up like foam. It was almost sinister. The pink cottages, lifting their roofs here and there above the hedges, seemed in danger of total immersion.

They passed a ruined abbey, gaunt walls standing amid neat, clipped grass.

"That's Cleeve Abbey," said Kester. "Have you been there? There's a place where one of the old monks drew a picture on the wall of one of the others, for a giggle. Brother Somebody, with a squashed nose and a bald head, like a cartoon. It's funny."

They crossed the main road, with traffic streaming nose to tail between Taunton and Minehead, and began to crawl through the last bit of hilly countryside before the coast. The bus stopped in every village: people got on and off, Kester talked. At last, as the bus climbed a steep hill, he got up. "We'll get off at the top. There's not a stop but he'll let us off. Otherwise we go down to Watchet and have to climb the hill again."

Deposited at the roadside, Lucy could smell the sea.

Somewhere near, there was the cry of gulls, infinitely mournful. They climbed a gate, and in front of them a field rolled down to the top of steep cliffs. Beyond that, the flat, cold grey of the Bristol Channel fused into a pale sky. The water was still, carven, ridged here and there by the wind.

"Do we have to climb down those cliffs?"

"There's a path, and you have to slide a bit here and there. Otherwise it's through the caravan site."

They descended steeply through a copse which clung precariously to the hillside, the saplings growing at an angle of forty-five degrees. It was cool, full of foxgloves and willowherb, skeins of midges hanging in the shafts of light. Below that again the ground fell away still more steeply, with rabbit tracks winding among gorse bushes. They slithered on the stones. Below them, the beach was grey, empty.

"I thought it was sand," said Lucy.

"That's further on, nearer Minehead. Iced lollies and a million people. This is where the fossils are."

The last bit was perpendicular. Lucy slid on her bottom, shrieking, and came to a halt on a ledge above a six-foot drop.

"This is where we jump."

"I can't."

"Don't be a nit!"

They landed together in a heap, clattering on the pebbles. The beach was like a vast, cobbled street. The smooth stones bit into their feet, sliding and shifting with every step. The cliffs rose up behind them, grey and shelving, veined here and there with pink.

"Alabaster," said Kester, picking up a lump of rock. Lucy took it from him: it was rose-coloured, dappled. She put it in her pocket.

"Where are the fossils, then?"

"Everywhere. You just have to look."

They scrunched among the stones, eyes to the ground. Presently Kester stopped. "Here's one."

It was like a little grey wheel, ridged, winding into itself. "Gosh! What is it?"

"Ignorant! It's an ammonite. Middle Liassic, I should think. Don't you know anything?"

Presently Lucy found a section of another. "I say! This one must have been about a yard big!"

"You get them even bigger sometimes. We'll have to leave that one—we can't lug it back."

They found things like delicate stone snails, scallop shells embedded in blocks of stone, and innumerable sections of ammonites, perfect in their symmetry. They filled their pockets; the hunt became obsessive, they moved over the beach like sheep-walkers, greedily acquisitive.

At last Kester said, "That'll do, I'm lumbered." His pockets sagged, clattering.

They sat down on a shoulder of rock, staring across the still water.

"You know, I did remember you—that time at Uncle Tom's. But I wasn't letting on. I thought you were a mate of those two girls."

"I felt awful," said Lucy, "as though I'd waved to someone in the street, and they'd turned their back or something."

"Sorry; I really am."

"I know. It's all right now."

"It's just I can't stand those two. Or their mum. So if you were one of them I just didn't want to know."

"Well, I'm not."

"No. You're not quite so thick. Though, I must say, someone who's never heard of Middle Liassic..." He squinted sideways at her, grinning.

"I bet you hadn't until you started your project or whatever it is," said Lucy indignantly. "As a matter of fact I'm rather well-informed. Stop laughing, or I'll—I'll..."

"Go on. You'll what?"

"I'll tell those boys you brought me here. The ones you're always squabbling with."

"You wouldn't, you know."

"No," said Lucy, subsiding. "You're quite right. I wouldn't."

"Anyway, I'm not that bothered. About them, I mean. It passes the time for all of us. It's not serious. Though it's true I'm not mates with them as when we were all at the same school."

"Not being able to talk any more," said Lucy. "Like me with Caroline and Louise."

"Yes, I s'pose so. You know something? We're a bit the same, you and me. We can't talk to people. We're kind of all shut up inside ourselves."

"My father says I'm gloomy."

"No. It's just that you know you're on your own, see? We all are, aren't we, really? But some people never seem to know it. Or else they're not bothered."

A dog trotted across the foreshore, its fawn and cream coat vivid against the uniform grey of the stones. Lucy watched it pass. The wind lifted her hair and brushed warm on her bare arms.

"You should be able to see Wales. That's Cardiff over there. Sometimes you can see the smoke from the steelworks up the coast."

But today the horizon was invisible in the curtain of grey that stretched from the water's edge in a great arc to the cliffs behind.

"I just thought, you're by yourself at your auntie's, aren't you? Why isn't your mum here?"

Lucy took one of the stone snails from her pocket. It curled into her palm, cool and smooth. "She doesn't live with us any more. She married someone else. My dad'll be coming later, when he gets his holiday."

"Oh, I see." Kester scowled at the sea for a moment. He put his hand in his pocket, tipped the fossils on a flat stone, and looked them over carefully. Then he picked out the one perfect ammonite.

"Here, you can have this one."

"Oh, Kester, it's the best."

"I know. Take it."

They took their shoes off and splashed through the sea-weed at the water's edge. Flat brown ribbons clutched at their feet and stuck like bands of plaster when they came out. They climbed over mounds and hillocks of the stuff, dried crisp by the sun and wind. At last Kester said, "We ought to go or we'll miss the last bus."

They walked slowly back to the path. Part of the cliff had crumbled away in the winter and lay in fragments at the base, like a broken slice cut from a great cake, exposing a stretch of raw, unweathered rock and earth.

"Look," said Kester, pointing.

"What?"

"In the cliff face. A shape like an animal. A head, and a long, long body, and a tail."

Lucy stared: "A dinosaur?"

"Could be."

They stood still, looking. The shape in the rock took form, quite clear—head, tail, knobbed backbone, and then, if you looked away, and looked back again, it was gone, melted into the layers of the cliff.

"Are we really seeing it?" said Lucy, "or are we just thinking it?"

"I dunno. Either. But it's funny it's the same for both of us."

"Like shapes in clouds. What do you see? Now?"

"Fish. A castle. An enormous face."

"Horses, with riders, and dogs running behind."

"No!" said Kester violently. He began to run towards the path, leaving her to scramble after him.

He was waiting for her at the bottom of the wood.

"Take your time, don't you?"

"It's your fault. I could hardly get up the bit at the bottom."

"You're soft. You shouldn't live in a town all the time." But he was laughing again, teasing. They ran through the wood and across the field, Lucy panting to keep up.

Waiting for the bus, Lucy said, "What about this fête thing?"

"Oh, that. It's a bun fight for the Vicar and Mrs. Whatsit and all them, mostly. But it's not so bad, really. My mum has a whale of a time. She does the cake stall—it's her big day."

"Do you help?"

"Not likely. I just come along for the laughs."

"I was there when they were talking about this Dance. I thought it was a bit creepy."

"Tell me. Was that what Mrs. Whatsit was talking about? I didn't really know what she was on about—just that if it was some lark of hers then I didn't want it anyway."

Lucy explained. Kester listened, intent. As she described the Vicar's appearance with the mask held to his face, the boy became very still, his face frozen, staring.

"Caroline laughed. I didn't. There was something nasty about it. What's the matter, Kester?"

He shook himself, blinked. "Oh, nothing. You just reminded me of something, that's all. So that's what that mask thing's for."

"Why? Have you seen it?"

"Once, just. In the vestry."

"When?"

"Oh, look, it doesn't matter." He stared up the road. The gulls wheeled above them, screaming.

"Please tell me."

"It was when I was very young—three or four, I dunno. I was in the church with my mum when she was helping decorate for the Harvest Festival, and there was some of the bigger boys there and they found this thing in a cupboard and one of them stuck it over his face and they crept up on me and chased me. I howled fit to burst, I can tell you. Funny, I can see it now, the way his eyes looked through the holes."

"I know," said Lucy.

The bus was throbbing in the distance, climbing the hill.

"How many of them do this Dance?"

"Twelve. I think it's a daft idea."

"Mmn. I s'pose so. Might be funny, though. I reckon I'll take a look."

When they arrived back at Hagworthy Kester said, "Have you got any books to spare? I could do with a break from Mesozoic fossils and the Tudors and Stuarts."

"Lots. Come and choose."

They went into the cottage together. Lucy left Kester in the hall while she went out into the garden through the back door to look for her aunt. The garden was empty, except for Whitby, stretched out asleep in the shade. He opened one eye when he heard her, and closed it again at once. She decided that Aunt Mable must be out plant-collecting somewhere and went back into the house.

Her rubber-soled shoes made no sound on the stone floor. Kester did not hear her coming. He was standing in a kind of trance, staring at the antlers on the wall with an excited fascination, as though they were something he had never seen before.

FOUR

LUCY BORROWED HER aunt's bicycle and rode with Kester along the dark road through the woods beyond Hagworthy and then up the long winding lane to the top, pushing the bikes side by side, with the steep banks arching above them, and freewheeling down, the wind whistling through the spokes and the bright hedges rushing past. They swam in the pool where the stream widened out into a shingled beach, gasping at the cold of the water, dragging their feet through the silken mud of the stream's bed.

They walked in the woods, waist deep in bracken and the spires of willow-herb, with the sunlight spitting and crackling through the roof of leaves far above their heads. They put sandwiches in haversacks and went for day-long expeditions, up over the Brendons and along the straight, bleak road across the top, with the distant glimpses of Devon flashing at them through gateways, through Dunster Park by Timberscombe to Wootton Courtney; up over silent stretches of moor and down through dark combes full of rushing water and dappled light.

Trees gave them shelter from the wind and the burning

sun, they drank from streams that came down from the moor and rested on beds of bracken like the deer. They forgot the time, and knew only by the quality of the light glowing on trees and grass when it was evening. They lost themselves, and learned to distinguish landmarks in the rise and fall of the hills, the shape of the fields, the distribution of trees. Lucy quarried in the hedgerows for wild flowers, and made Kester list the names for her. They watched birds, traced a badger's path from his sett under a hedge, talked, slept, ate and talked again. In the evenings Lucy sat dazed with fresh air and exhaustion, propped in a chair staring vacantly at the book in her hand, seeing again the branches of trees streaming above her and that whole, various landscape stretching away under a sky ridged with grey cloud.

One or twice they caught sight of Caroline and Louise in the distance, and fled behind hedges. Lucy, unable to refuse an invitation issued formally over the telephone to Aunt Mabel, went to the house for tea and spent an uneasy afternoon, battered by Mrs. Norton-Smith's relentless enthusiasm.

"You must come to the village hall on Saturday evening, Lucy. We're rehearsing for the Dance. It's all right if Lucy comes to watch, isn't it, Mummy?"

"My dear, we shall have half the village watching. The more the merrier."

"It's a shame you can't be in it, Lucy. But it's a bit difficult. I mean, so many of the village people want to — they might be hurt if we let visitors do it."

"I don't mind, honestly."

"Actually I think really the Vicar wanted to be in it, but he thought he oughtn't to. It might be a bit undignified."

"Such a good sport, that man," said Mrs. Norton-Smith. "Not a bit stuffy."

* * *

Lucy sitting with Kester at the back of the forge, watching Mr. Hancock hammer out iron for shoes, passed on the information. She was wary of the smith, a little nervous. He was a man in whom moods succeeded each other with bewildering variety, humour giving way to sudden snatches of anger, a communicating moment to unexplained irritation. Lucy thought she could see something of him reflected in Kester: was this perhaps why they grated on one another? But there was no physical resemblance between them. Kester was thin, sparrow-light, bony as a colt: the smith was a man hewn from rock itself, slow and deliberate. Only their eyes held a common awareness, the same watchful stare.

They talked of the Dance.

"What?" said Kester. "The Vicar? You must be joking! I mean, it's not very Christian, all this stuff, is it?"

The smith chuckled. "Church were always for the Dance, in the old days. She had to, see. It were part of the old things. When she couldn't stop 'em, she had to take 'em up, didn't she? To show she were on top, like."

Lucy said, trying to sound casual, "Is it very old, then?"

"Look girl, there was dancing in the combe afore the Church ever were thought of. There was dancing here when the fairies were still up in the hills."

"The fairies!" said Kester. "Don't make me laugh, Uncle! And the piskies too, I suppose?"

"I'm not laughing, boy, I'm *telling* you. And you know it, but you're not saying in front of the girl, are you?" Kester turned away, scowling.

The smith began to work the bellows. The sinking fire glowed, and presently flames burst up and sent long, forked shapes licking up towards the roof.

"And then they stopped it because they'd grown afraid of the Hunt, and they thought the one brought the other."

He chuckled again, thrusting the iron into the fire and turning it in the flames.

"The Hunt?" said Lucy, in a whisper.

"That's it girl, the Hunt. Why are you asking? Are you afraid too? It were a great thing, once, the Hunt. Nothing to be afraid of. It were a splendid thing, though not for a man to look on with his eyes. But folk have grown smaller. They be afraid of it now. Eh, Kester?"

"It's a load of old rubbish," said Kester savagely. "This is the twentieth century, in case you hadn't noticed, Uncle. We've got jet planes, and computers, and all that. Ever noticed they use tractors round here now, and combine harvesters?"

"You can say what you like, boy. You know how things are, well as I do. It's not thrown off by clever talk."

"Oh come on, Lucy, I've had enough. Let's go and swim."

On their way to the stream Lucy said, "What does your uncle mean? Sometimes he makes me feel funny, the way he talks."

"Look, you don't want to take too much notice. He's never set foot out of Hagworthy in his life, Uncle Tom, except for Taunton Races once a year. He goes on at me because they wanted me to work at the forge, and I'm not going to."

"What do you want to do?"

"I dunno. But not stay here, I know that. I mean, it's great—it's home—but it won't do for me all the time, when I'm older, I know that for sure."

The weather had taken a turn for the better. It was hot, the sky bare of clouds and arching blue over the countryside. The corn ripened, the trees were dusky in the heat haze and the dry earth pink and cracked. It was good to plunge into the cool stream and drift in the shade of the bank, looking upwards at the buttercups shimmering on the edge and through the trembling green of the aspens overhanging the river.

"I wish now was for ever," said Lucy. "I want to be here like this for always and always." There was a bloom of sunlight on the water, quivering.

"You'd look pretty silly in the winter. Drifting there like that with icebergs all round you."

"I wouldn't care. I'd be like the water-rats—I wouldn't feel the hot or the cold."

Mayflies skimmed, level with her head, and water-boatmen ran on the surface of the water, their feet leaving minute dimples as though on molten glass. Mysterious movements under water tickled her feet: tugging of weeds, the delicate flick of minnows.

"There's a fish biting my feet."

"You don't say!"

"Ouch! That must have been a big one."

"You want to watch it. There's been pike in here."

Something nipped, sharper. "Oh, Kester, help—honestly, there is something! Oh, gosh..."

Laughter.

"Oh, Kester, it was you! Oh, you beast!" The water thrashed, the reflections shattered into jigsaws of light. "Just wait till I get you..."

They lay on the grass and slept in the sun, with the cows munching and swishing around them.

On Saturday evening, Lucy sat on the wall and watched the progress of the Fête organizers towards the Village Hall. The Norton-Smiths drove down in their car, the back piled high with costumes, antlers strapped absurdly to the roof-rack. The girls waved at Lucy. The Vicar passed on foot, carrying musical instruments and an armful of papers. Other people drifted by, children, women in twos and threes, men in shirt sleeves with hands thrust in trouser pockets, deliberately casual. She waited for Kester, and they went down together.

The Village Hall was a long, low building next to the garage. There was a small car park in front, gay with tubs of geraniums and petunias, and behind the recreation ground, with football pitch and swings and slides, stretched right across the narrow floor of the valley.

"Hello, Lucy," said Mrs. Norton-Smith. "Come to see the fun?" She ignored Kester.

They selected a vantage point on a window-sill with their feet resting on a radiator, and settled down to watch. The hall was gradually filling, the spectators sitting round the walls on folding chairs, chattering in pleasurable anticipation, the organizers and Dancers milling about in the centre of the floor. On the stage at the end, Mrs. Norton-Smith was dispensing costumes, amid shrieks of laughter.

"What's this, then? Me gran's old combinations?"

"Actually, they're meant to be kind of medieval stockings," explained Caroline earnestly. "Tights, really. We're not sure, you see, what they wore exactly in the old days, but we thought it must be something like this."

"Let's have a look at you, Rosie. Oh, you do look funny, love!"

"Are we supposed to be men or women?" said someone plaintively. "You can't tell no difference, with them breeches."

"Ah," said the Vicar, "now that's a good point. The records aren't at all clear about that, but I have a sort of feeling the Dance was usually done by men or boys."

"Well, we're six of each."

"Never mind. Since we're a bit hazy about what actually did go on in Hagworthy I've been doing a bit of research into these folk dances and we're modelling it more or less on the Abbot's Bromley one. Now, we want six dancers, and then we've got a few leading roles. There's the Fool, and the Man-woman, and the Hobby-horse, and three musicians. Someone to twang this bow thing—borrowed from the Museum, actually, so we've got to be awfully careful of it—and the chap with the drum, and a flute player. Now, who's going to be the Fool?"

There was much laughter and suggestion. Finally a red-faced lad of fifteen or so was pushed forward, protesting violently.

"Good for you, Tom," said Mrs. Norton-Smith enthusiastically. "That's the stuff!" She crammed a stocking-cap on to his head. Kester thrust his head into his hands, his shoulders heaving.

A hefty boy who worked at the garage was cast as the Man-woman, and dressed by Mrs. Norton-Smith in a long hessian skirt and a veil borrowed from a local bee-keeper. The spectators roared their approval, and he took a few mincing steps round the Hall.

"Actually this is really a rather interesting survival," said the Vicar, with a hint of rebuke in his voice, "not entirely to be made fun of. Not that I want to spoil anyone's pleasure."

Lucy and Kester were clutching each other convulsively, shaking with suppressed laughter.

"Now, who's going to be our flautist?"

Caroline's hand shot up. "Can I have a go? I learned the recorder at school once?"

"Good show. D'you think you could manage the drum, Margaret? Good girl. And what about you with the bow thing, John? It's just a case of plucking it, apparently, nothing fancy."

"Can I be Hobby-horse, Vicar?"

It was a brawny, bull-necked boy with a thatch of ginger

hair, the son of the pub owner. The Vicar looked a little unenthusiastic. "Yes, very well, Jim."

The Hobby-horse was something like the old-fashioned child's toy, wood-carved and mounted on a stick. "Here you are," said the Vicar. "Not awfully authentic, I'm afraid. Mrs. Notley made it for us. As far as I can make out they used a horse's skull in the old days, but we thought that was a bit unpleasant."

"Beastly," said Caroline, shuddering.

Jim Thacker seized the Hobby-horse and began careering round the hall, charging into the groups of girls round the walls, who scattered shrieking.

"Yes, that'll do, Jim," said the Vicar. "We don't want to get carried away, do we?" He turned to Mrs. Norton-Smith and murmured in an undertone: "We'll have to keep an eye on that lad—we don't want any hooliganism."

Mrs. Norton-Smith clapped her hands. "Right—everyone know what they are now? Now, the thing is, the Vicar's going to run through the steps—so far as we're at all sure what they did. So shall we get going? All the Dancers in the middle of the Hall, please. Everyone else out of the way."

The Dancers shuffled self-consciously into the centre of the floor, amid derisory encouragement from the spectators. It was dusk outside now. Through the windows Lucy could see the string of naked bulbs above the garage glittering against the darkening sky.

"Can't we have lights on?" shouted someone.

"Good idea!" said Mrs. Norton-Smith. "Can't see a thing. Someone put them on, please."

The lights snapped on and the Dancers, bathed in the harsh glare, blinked and giggled.

"Now," said the Vicar, climbing up on the stage, "two lines facing each other, please, six aside."

"Does it matter who goes where?" said Caroline anxiously.

"Er . . . I think not. Perhaps we'll have the Man-woman and the Fool at the top, and the musicians at the other end. And then later when you get in single file—I'll tell you when—the Hobby-horse should lead. He's supposed to snap his jaws and run into the crowd, and that sort of thing, you know. But don't overdo it, eh, Jim?"

The Hobby-horse said something inaudible and a bunch of girls near by giggled hysterically.

"Ssh!" said Mrs. Norton-Smith.

"Right. All ready? Now the step is just a sort of hop and a skip. Like this. Quite simple. Remember you're going to be doing it for a long time, on the day, right round the village and up the combe and back here again. So everyone's got to be frightfully fit and in training. But to begin with you set to the person opposite, like in Scottish dancing, one after the other, starting with the pair at the top; and then you make a single file and the leader doubles back through the line, in and out. Got it?"

"Reckon so," said the Man-woman. "What about them antlers, though?"

"Good gracious!" said the Vicar. "We've forgotten the most important part."

The antlers, mounted on short sticks, were piled in a heap at the foot of the stage. Several spectators jumped up and helped give them out to the Dancers.

"You hold them with both hands," said the Vicar, "so the masks cover your faces. It's going to be a bit tiring on the arms, I'm afraid."

The twelve Dancers raised the antlers. They reached above their heads, throwing huge shadows on the floor behind them. The masks blotted out their faces, only their eyes showing through the sockets, so that suddenly they were anonymous and indistinguishable one from another, strange mythical creatures, half-human and half animal. Lucy gave a startled gasp and at the same moment there was a sharp crack from somewhere outside and all the lights went out.

Some of the girls shrieked. The Dancers stood still, only their outlines visible in the gloom: a monstrous, misplaced group.

"Bother!" said Mrs. Norton-Smith, "the electricity's gone again."

"All right," said the Vicar. "No good trying to go on now. You can put the antlers down, Dancers. We'll have to go through it again next week."

The Dancers broke up, pulling off their costumes and talking. Lucy, peering at them as her eyes became accustomed to the darkness, was relieved to see once again their familiar, ordinary faces. She turned to Kester, who had been silent for some time, and saw that he was no longer laughing, but staring in a kind of dazed bewilderment at the group of boys stacking their masks and antlers at the side of the Hall.

Later, she said to Aunt Mabel, in the candle-lit quietness of the cottage, "Does the electricity often go off?"

"Frequently," said Aunt Mabel. "It's never been reliable in Hagworthy."

"They rehearsed this Dance thing this evening. The lights went out in the middle and it was—well, ever so odd. You could only see the shapes of them."

"And who are they—the Dancers?"

"Oh, the teenagers, mostly. Boys. And a few girls, and Caroline. Louise is too short. The boy from the pub. People like that. The Vicar wanted to but he isn't because it might be undignified."

"Really?" said Aunt Mabel, "one can't help wishing he was. That would have been most interesting. However..."

Peering in the light of the candle, Lucy wrote to her father.

> I am having a very good time at Aunt Mabel's. She is not quite what I expected, but nicer. I have seen Caroline and Louise sometimes but they are very interested in ponies now. I go bicycling with Kester and it is lovely going fast downhill on the way back. We went to the beach and we thought we saw a dinosaur in the cliff and he gave me the best ammonite—Kester, I mean. They are doing a queer sort of Dance in the village for a Fête, with antlers and masks. I love Aunt Mabel's cottage, except for the picture on the stairs. I must stop now because the candle is nearly burnt out (this is because the electricity went off). It is very hot here. Love from Lucy.

Hagworthy remained plunged in darkness that night. Thunder roamed the sky, so that Lucy lay awake for a long time, hot, with the sheets thrown back, listening to the angry sky noises and waiting for the refreshing rain that never came. At last she fell asleep, but woke again an hour or two later with a start. The thunder had ceased, but the combe was full of noise. A wind had sprung up and was rattling the windows and pushing a dustbin lid up and down the alley beyond the cottage. There were other sounds too—the whisper of the trees in the fields above and something that might have been the pattering of leaves. Restless, she got out of bed and went on to the landing, where she stood uneasily, looking down into the dark well of the hall for a few minutes. There seemed to be something wrong, and she went back to bed dissatisfied. Only in the morning did it occur to her what it was.

"Aunt Mabel, did you lend any of your antlers to the Fête people?"

"No. Nobody asked me."

"Last night in the middle of the night there were only three lots there instead of four."

"I can't imagine why you should take it upon yourself to count antlers in the middle of the night, child. However, let us investigate."

They went into the hall: eight antlers, one with Aunt Mabel's gardening hat perched jauntily on its points.

"I'm sure . . ." said Lucy, confused. "At least, I thought I was sure."

Aunt Mabel patted her kindly. "I daresay you were. Anyway, it's hardly anything to get worked up about. Are you going to go down to the shop for me?"

It was hot again. The road was sticky with melting tar, the stream shrinking a little between its banks instead of running high against the grass. In the fields, the red cows were drawn into huddled groups under the trees. The hedgerows hummed with flies.

Lucy had to wait in the shop while the other customers were served. There were two old women, talking.

"Heavy, today."

"Yes, we could do with a drop o' rain now."

"Is it true they were out in the night? I didn't hear nothing."

"That's so. They come down from the hill, and through the combe, like they always did. I heard, but I didn't look out, not I."

"It's been a long time."

"Best if it had stayed that way."

They looked at Lucy as they left, with a hard unselfconscious stare like that of small children.

She met Kester as she was on the way back to the cottage,

spinning stones on the surface of the stream, apparently in a high good humour.

"That was a good laugh last night, wasn't it?"

"I didn't like it when the lights went out. It was scary, almost."

"Don't be daft! Jim Thacker and that lot? Scary! Don't make me laugh!"

"It's those masks. You can't tell who anyone is."

"That's right," said Kester, suddenly abstracted, "nor you can." He stared at her, deep in thought.

"What's up, Kester? You might tell me."

"Nothing. Look, there's an old water-rat got a hole down there. I've been watching him for hours. There—he's putting his face out again."

Lucy put the basket down and leaned over the wall. The dark water ran a foot or two under their faces, full of another, secret life.

"Fish—look, under the bank. Is it a trout?"

"Could be. I say, we'll get my old rod out after dinner and go further up."

They were so engrossed that they did not hear the clatter of hooves behind them.

"Hello, Lucy," said Caroline, with a disapproving look at Kester. "Did you enjoy it last night?" She was walking, leading a big brown horse.

"Pony's grown a bit, hasn't it?" said Kester.

"Oh, this is Mummy's mare. I've got to bring her in because she's going to foal any day and Mummy doesn't want to have to keep trailing up the hill to look at her."

"It looks like it's going to have triplets at least," said Kester.

"That's stupid. Horses don't. Even twins is pretty unusual."

"Forgive my ignorance."

"Gosh, isn't it hot! Honestly, I must have a rest before I pass out." She perched herself on the wall. The horse began to crop grass at the roadside.

"What are you looking at?"

"Oh, nothing really," said Lucy.

"Honestly, you are funny, Lucy. I was watching you and you were just staring and staring at the water. And yesterday we went past and you were sitting on your aunt's wall with a book and we shouted like mad and you didn't even look up. Mummy says she's never known such a dreamy girl."

"Mummy doesn't know much."

"Actually I wasn't talking to you, Kester. We're going to be here all day if you'd like to come up later, Lucy. Mummy says it's a pity we don't see more of you. I s'pose I'd better go now."

When she had gone Lucy said, "You don't have to be quite so rude. She's not all that bad, really. She can't help being like that."

"Can't she just! All right. Sorry."

"You do get in a rage about people, Kester. Them, and the other boys—the ones you're always arguing with. Why bother so much about them?"

"Look, I don't."

"You do. I saw you yesterday with the boy from the pub and those others. Arguing, and shouting at each other."

"Well, it's because I like it, then. Anyway, Jim Thacker's thick."

"I hate arguing with people. I just go away."

"Good old you, then," said Kester, bored. "Let's go and get my rod now. Matter of fact I think it may be bust anyway. I haven't had it out since last year."

Kester's cottage adjoined the smithy. His mother was in the kitchen, peeling potatoes at the sink.

"We've come for my rod, Mum."

"It'll be upstairs, in the old wardrobe. You wait down here, love, while he gets it."

Lucy sat at the kitchen table.

"Enjoying your holidays?"

"I'll say—I wish they'd go on for ever. It's like it was years ago, really, when we were younger. Kester's going to take me up on the moor at dawn soon so we can see the deer."

"Oh yes? It's a good thing for Kester, having you here. He's not got so many friends in the village now he goes to the Grammar. He's changed this last year or two."

Kester came clattering down the narrow stairs. "The line's rotted, Mum. What can I use?"

"You'd best see your uncle about it. He'll likely have something that'll do."

They went through the side door into the forge. The dark figure of the smith stood among the leaping shadows from the furnace.

"Uncle Tom? You got anything I can have for a fishing line?"

"Oh, it's you, is it? I been wondering when you'd show your face. Well, did you hear it?"

"Hear what?"

"The Hunt, boy. I told you there'd be hunting, didn't I? They was out in the night."

Kester scowled angrily. "Look, I've had enough of that, Uncle. Joke over, eh?"

"What's up, boy? Frightened, are you?"

"Me? I'm not frightened." The boy spoke with suppressed fury, his thin face white, eyes blazing.

"That's right. You got no need to be. That's for other folk, eh? Now, what's this about a fishing-line?"

Later, walking up the combe to the wider part of the

stream, Lucy said, "I wish your uncle would stop it. Going on about this Hunt."

"Shut up! Just shut up, see!"

Tears pricked her eyes. She trailed after him, slapping the flies that stung her arms and legs, choking with the sickly smell of the meadowsweet.

FIVE

"ACTUALLY MUMMY SAYS it was all rather beastly really and she'd rather not talk about it. So don't say anything."

"What exactly was it like?" said Lucy.

"We don't really know. Pretty horrid, I think. The vet came early and tidied everything up before we got up. Poor Mummy was up most of the night. The mare's all right, though."

"Did it have two heads or something?"

"Oh, do shut up, Lucy. We don't want to think about it any more. Mrs. Webb would keep going on and Mummy got fed up and had to tell her to be quiet. The village people can be awfully tiresome and superstitious sometimes. I mean, you often get calves and foals and things born not right and it's just rotten luck and you have to forget about it. But it got Mummy all upset and we've had a perfectly foul morning, so don't you start too."

"Sorry, Caroline."

"I say, did you know we're rehearsing the Dance tonight? In the recreation ground this time, like it'll be on the day. Let's hope it doesn't pour."

"Doesn't look like it," said Lucy.

It was too hot. By midday the air quivered with heat as the sun climbed in a hard blue sky. Shadows lay under trees and hedges like dark puddles. In the fields the barley was stiff and motionless. Aunt Mabel discarded her tweed skirt and put on an ancient, creased cotton dress. She sat in a deck chair in front of the cottage, with Whitby panting underneath it.

"Where's Kester today?"

"I don't know."

He came in the early afternoon, peering cautiously round the gate. Lucy, nursing deep offence, read her book and squinted over the top of the page.

"Hello."

Silence.

"Look, I'm sorry about yesterday. I just got a bit fed up, see. It didn't mean anything."

"All right, then."

"Go on, smile. Look, have I shown you my Vicar face? Dearly beloved, here we are gathered together . . ."

"Oh, Kester, you are daft!"

"That's better. What are we doing, then?"

"It's too hot to move."

"You can't stay sat there all day. You'll grow roots. We'll go up on the hill. Cooler up there."

On the hill they waded through bracken up to their waists, like swimmers in a green sea. They lay on their backs deep in the heart of it and stared up at the curling fronds, clean and sharp against the sky, delicate as the snail shapes of fossils. Birds floated above them, their wings translucent. Larks sang, invisible, miles up in the blue heights of the sky.

"Hey, Kester, there's been someone else here. The bracken's all flattened."

"Not people, silly."

"What, then?"

"There's been a stag. Look, you can see the shape of him. Lying up in the heat. Yesterday, most likely."

"A stag?" She stared, wonderingly. "Might we see it?"

"Not this time of day. They stay hid, you see. You've got to get up early to see them. At dawn when they're feeding. I said I'd take you."

"When?"

"Tomorrow, maybe. Yes, tomorrow."

Lucy said, "People hunt them here, don't they? I think that's horrible. Killing things for the sake of killing them. It's different if it's things to eat."

"They do eat them."

"The stags?"

"That's right. It gets chopped up and different bits given to the farmers whose land it was hunted over. The one whose land it was found on gets one haunch, and the one whose land it died on gets another hunk and so on. And different people get the head and the feet."

"That's nasty," said Lucy. "Nasty and a bit peculiar. It's not straightforward eating, is it?"

"No. No, I s'pose it isn't. It's pretty odd, when you come to think about it."

"Have you ever done it? Hunting?"

"Me? You must be joking! I've seen it often enough, though. It's the big thing round here, after all."

"What's it like?"

"Oh, a great mob of people and horses. And the hounds. I don't mind them—the hounds. It's quite something when you see them spread out over the moor: it looks like a whole hill's running. Weird. But the people turn me up rather. When you start thinking of what it's all about, I mean."

Lucy nodded. She patted the crushed bracken. "Anyway, this one got away."

"Oh, they give them a break in the summer anyway. They have this ceremony on May 1st when the hunting stops, you see. It's called the Spring Truce and the huntsman and the farmers and all the Mrs. Norton-Smiths do this ceremonial dance round the War Memorial and declare that they won't hunt again till the harvest moon is full. It's very traditional, you see."

Lucy stared in amazement. "Goodness. That must be awfully queer."

"Oh, it's that all right. And then they sacrifice two hounds in front of Uncle Tom's forge."

"Oh, how cruel! Kester, you're laughing . . . Oh, you beast, you're having me on. I should have known . . ."

He lay face down in the bracken, shoulders heaving. Lucy's indignation dissolved and she began to giggle.

"All the same, I'd like to see Mrs. Norton-Smith doing a ceremonial dance."

They did not come down from the hill until the sun was low in the sky and the shadows long, streaming down the side of the combe. The light glowed with the intensity of early evening, the fields were sharply green, the trees soft with a grey bloom. But in the distance long clouds, like great fish, lay above the horizon.

"Reckon there could be a storm," said Kester. "That'll muck up their old Dance tonight."

"Are we going?"

"You bet."

"Kester, were you having me on about the stags too? About chopping them up like that?"

"No. Oh, no, that's real."

"How revolting. By the way, I meant to tell you—Caroline was all fussed this morning. That horse had its foal but it was dead, and sort of deformed or something."

"What?"

"The foal. There was something wrong with it. What's up, Kester? Why are you looking like that?"

"Nothing, it doesn't matter."

They ran the last half mile down to Hagworthy, shouting to each other and skidding on the loose gravel of the lane. It was hotter down there, like plunging into warm soup, as though the heat of the day were trapped between the shoulders of the hills. They stopped at the shop to buy ice-cream, and sat on the wall outside to eat them.

"Here comes Uncle Tom. Look, don't say anything about that horse."

"I wasn't going to. But why not?"

"Just don't, that's all."

The smith stopped beside them, tamping the tobacco in his pipe with a massive thumb. Then he tucked the pipe into the corner of his mouth and put his hands in his pockets.

"It's all very well for some, eh? Nothing to do but sit on their backsides and watch the world go by." He winked at Lucy.

"Some world!" said Kester. "Old Mrs. Taylor, the Summers kids, three dogs, and a chicken."

"And the bread van," said Lucy, "coming up the hill."

"Big deal."

"It were enough for me, boy, when I were a lad."

"I wasn't grumbling, Uncle. Just saying."

"Huh. I daresay. All the same, we were satisfied with less in my day. We weren't looking for trips to Mine'ead all the time, and shiny bikes like you boys has nowadays."

"I hate Minehead," said Kester. "All noise, and people in daft clothes."

"I been in Hagworthy all my life, and I daresay I'll die here, and I'm well satisfied."

Lucy gave Kester a nervous look, but he said, "Hagworthy's all right. I've never said it wasn't."

"All the same, boy, you've got an itch in you. You'll be off, one o' these days. But I'll tell you one thing." The smith took his pipe out of his mouth and pushed his face closer to Kester's: his skin, seen in close-up, was rudely pitted by sparks from the anvil: "I'll tell you one thing: you'll never shake off the place you've come from. It's what made you, and it stays inside of you, come what may. It's the same for all of us."

"I know," said Kester. He glanced at Lucy, and then looked away again quickly, whistling through his teeth, squinting against the sun, low behind the hill.

There was a pause. The smith smoked, seeming to be lost in contemplation.

Kester said to Lucy, "Come on, we'd better get something to eat before tonight."

"Eh? Tonight?"

"Just that old Dance of theirs, Uncle. We'll be going along. To watch—just for a laugh."

"You'd far better keep away from that. Keep right away."

"Why?" said Kester, staring.

"Don't ask, boy!" said the smith, with sudden violence, "just leave it alone, see."

"But what's the harm in going along to watch? It's a right laugh, Jim Thacker and them jumping about like a load of girls."

"I'm telling you. Leave it alone."

Kester seemed about to argue, but Lucy tugged his arm. "Kester—come *on*."

The smith said, "You tell him, girl. Tell him to leave it alone."

"All right, all right," said Kester. He and Lucy walked away down the road.

"What did he mean?" said Lucy.

"I dunno. It doesn't matter."

Most of the village seemed to be on the recreation ground, women and small children gathered round the swings at one end, boys and footballs eddied to and fro on the far side, a game of cricket was going on somewhere else, girls hung gossiping round the gate. As the Dancers emerged from the Hall in a self-conscious group, the spectators drifted together. Kester and Lucy secured themselves a vantage point at the top of the steps. Caroline came staggering out with a pile of costumes.

"Hey, we got to put them things on in this heat?"

"Oh, I don't know. I'll ask Mummy. P'raps we could start off as we are, just for the first run-through."

Around the field, the same exchanges took place a dozen times over. "Shocking hot day it's been . . ."

"Aye. We need rain now."

"You'd think the weather mattered, the way people go on about it," said Lucy.

"Well, doesn't it? If it rains you get wet."

"Only outside. It's what you're feeling inside that matters. It can be a lovely day and you feel perfectly miserable, so what's the weather got to do with it?"

"Yes, I see. But really they aren't talking to each other at all, are they? They're just opening their mouths and making noises."

"Aunt Mabel and I do that sometimes. We sit at each side of the table and say things at each other. I wish we didn't, because I like her."

"Mmn. I do that with my mum, too."

"What about your Uncle Tom?"

"Uncle Tom?" Kester snorted. "Oh, you can't help talking to him. Only it's more like shouting. Both of you as loud as you can, and the loudest one wins."

"You like him really, you know."

"That's what *you* think."

"All the same, you do."

"Huh!"

People were beginning to gather in a group around Mrs. Norton-Smith and her entourage.

"Mummy, is it all right if we start off just in our ordinary clothes? It's so hot."

The Vicar and Mrs. Norton-Smith both spoke together.

"Oh, no, I do think the costumes are essential for them to get the feel of the thing..."

"Oh, gosh, let them wear what they like. We don't want people passing out right and left!"

There was an awkward pause. "Just as you like, Mrs. Norton-Smith," said the Vicar, in an offended tone. "I had rather thought I was directing the Dancers."

But the Dancers had already moved off on to the grass and were forming up into two lines. The Vicar followed them.

"No need to get all huffy," said Mrs. Norton-Smith, not bothering to lower her voice. "I say, Louise, I've got this beastly headache again. Run and get me the aspirins from the car."

The Dance progressed slowly. The Dancers capered self-consciously, bumping into each other, giggling, the boys clowning to attract the attention of those spectators who had not already wandered away. Only Caroline skipped about, frowning and listening intently to the Vicar's instructions.

"No, I said the Hobby-horse to lead when you get into single file, not the Fool. And then he doubles back through the line, in and out."

"That's what I done, Vicar."

"Yes, but there's no need to bump into them all like that. It's an absolute shambles."

"It's they girls, Vicar. They sticks their feet out."

"Well, they'll have to space out more, and can't you try to get some sort of rhythm on that triangle. Look! Like this."

"He's not got the right touch with those boys," said Mrs. Norton-Smith in a loud voice. "Pity..."

The Vicar took out a handkerchief and wiped his forehead. "Look, Caroline's the only one who's got the little step right, with the bob at the end. Do it on your own, Caroline."

"We ain't all been to dancing classes," said the Man-woman loudly.

Caroline went pink.

"Really!" said Mrs. Norton-Smith.

Kester suddenly put his fingers in his mouth and let out a piercing whistle: "Come on, then, Jim Thacker, let's see you get stuck into it. Let's have some action."

The boy glared across the grass. "That's enough from you, young Lang," he shouted dangerously, "or I'll come and sort yer out, see?"

Kester whistled again, derisive.

"It's no good," said the Vicar, almost shouting, "the atmosphere's all wrong. They'll have to put the costumes on. And in any case they've got to practise with the antlers, to get used to holding them. We'll have ten minutes break while they all get ready." He went into the Hall, every red in the face, loosening his collar.

Mrs. Norton-Smith and Caroline started to hand out the costumes.

"I 'eard about your bit o' bad luck," said one of the older women.

"Yes," said Mrs. Norton-Smith, "well, never mind, these things happen."

"It were a queer thing to 'appen just now, I reckon. 'Tis a bad sign, a birth like that."

Mrs. Norton-Smith said shortly, "Unfortunate at any time. One doesn't like to lose a foal. Caroline, do think what you're doing, child. Those tights are much too small for Margaret."

A wall of purple cloud had built up behind the sharp rise of the hill, like some dramatic backcloth.

"Oy smell rain, oy do," said Kester. "Oy can feel 'un in the pricking of my thumbs. It do be like instinct, to us country folk."

"Don't show off," said Lucy.

"There be thunder in the air."

"Anyone can see that, idiot."

At last the Dancers were ready. The Vicar returned. "Right. Now could everybody take up their antlers."

The Hobby-horse and the Man-woman already had. They were at the far end of the football pitch, carrying on a mock fight, watched by a group of shrieking girls. The wooden clicks as the antlers struck each other were very loud in the still evening.

The Vicar shouted: "I said, we're all ready!"

"Come on, man," said Mrs. Norton-Smith in a loud whisper. "Let's have a bit more discipline."

At last the Dancers were reassembled. The sky was very dark now, the clouds massing above the combe. Most of the spectators had gone home. The Dancers' costumes were bright, red, blue, yellow, orange—against the sharp green of the grass.

"It is weird," said Lucy. "I don't think they realize."

Kester did not answer and she turned to look at him. He

was very white, his eyes huge and dark, staring over the grass. His hands twitched on his knees.

"What's the matter, Kester? Do you feel all right?"

He snapped at her, "Of course I do."

Lucy, injured, was silent, though from time to time she glanced at him. He seemed to have forgotten about her in his absorption with the Dance.

"Once right through," said the Vicar, "with the music. And for heaven's sake try to keep the beat. And then you lead off, Hobby-horse, out through the car park and towards the road, like we'll be doing on the day. But stop, of course, when you get to the road."

The Dance began. Suddenly, the clowning stopped. The two rows of figures skipped and swayed, faceless behind the masks, the antlers dipping and soaring above their heads, without grace but with a strange archaic dignity. For the moment, their individual personalities had vanished, merged in a collective activity that set them quite apart from the watchers at the edge of the field. They seemed to be alone in the dark stillness of the valley, beneath the lowering sky, alone and a thousand years old. The only sounds were the brush of their feet on the grass, the rhythmic thrum and twang of the instruments, and the ceaseless flow of the stream behind. They hinted at a memory of a thousand other summer twilights, as though something the valley held were released, expressed in the strange ritual of the Dance. Lucy shivered and clutched her bare arms.

And then suddenly, light flared in the sky, picking out for a second the branching shapes of the antlers. Thunder roared, right overhead, and almost immediately came the first warm drops of rain.

"Oh dear," said the Vicar, "we do seem fated with these rehearsals. All right, Dancers, fall out."

Some of the Dancers hesitated uncertainly, and then ran towards the Hall, letting their masks fall. But Jim Thacker and the other boys were careering wildly off in the direction of the road, charging like bulls, and shouting. The Vicar went after them, calling ineffectually.

"I said we'd have trouble with that boy," said Mrs. Norton-Smith. "Bit of a mistake to let him take part, really. Let's hope the Vicar can handle it."

Lucy turned towards Kester, and found herself alone. He had vanished without a word. Feeling resentful, she set off to go back to the cottage. Jim Thacker and the others were still rampaging up the street in the dusk—weird, berserk figures stamping and waving their antlers, black shapes against the shining wet surface of the tarmac and the pale walls of the cottages. Children shrieked in delighted terror, and old women at their doors muttered disapprovingly. There was no sign of the Vicar.

And then Kester appeared, a thin figure running catfooted along the top of the churchyard wall, taunting the Dancers. Insults and laughter floated back down the street to Lucy, and the anger of Jim Thacker, raging below like a frustrated bull. Suddenly Kester jumped from the wall and fled over a stile and into a field, and they stormed after him, clumsy hampered figures in their costumes, the antlers like weapons in their hands. It was absurd, and something else besides. People stared and some laughed.

"They boys! They be always foolin' about."

"It ain't all foolin' mind. They be after Kester Lang, some o' them. It seems like he don't fit in with the other lads no more."

"Vicar don't know what he's doing, bringing back the Dance. It do seem to make things worse."

But Lucy stared at the dark shapes running over the grass, and the fleeing figure of Kester, easily outstripping his pursuers, laughing at them over his shoulder, until he vanished into the trees, and then she went home, disturbed, as the thunder rumbled in the far corners of the sky and warm rain pattered on the roofs. She took special care to avoid looking at the picture as she went up to bed, but even so she dreamed uneasily in the night—dreams in which Kester drowned in some suffocating sea while she looked on helpless, and forked shapes made a pattern like the branches of trees on his staring face.

Pebbles spat against the window and woke her. She pulled the curtain back and saw Kester standing in the garden, in the flat grey light of dawn.

"Are you coming? It's gone five."

"Just a minute." She pulled on clothes, ran a comb through her hair, and went down, collecting a hunk of bread from the kitchen on the way. Whitby gave her a look of mild astonishment and went to sleep again.

"Will we really see a stag?"

"Can't promise. But we might."

Kester had got her bike out of the shed and was waiting in the lane. They set off without a word on the long pull up the valley, Kester riding ahead, whistling softly to himself. There was no sun yet, but the combe glowed with a soft light, and hummed with noise and life. Wood-pigeons rumbled and crashed in the trees by the road, the hedges were alive with birds, the fields full of munching cattle. It was as though all the business of the day must be crammed into these brief hours of the early morning.

As the incline grew steeper they got off and pushed the bikes. Kester turned once and said over his shoulder, "All right? It's a long pull up."

"Yes, thanks."

They trudged on in silence, heads down now, panting a

little, the hedges high on either side of them. At last the lane petered out at a gate, with a sweep of open common on the far side.

"This is where we leave the bikes," said Kester.

They went through the gate and began to walk through bracken, still climbing the shoulder of the moor. The ordered pattern of fields lay behind them now, giving way to the rougher green and brown reach of Exmoor, stretching away on every side in long slack lines against the clear sky, the hills tucking down here and there into the deep folds of combes lined with dark trees.

"Where are we going?" said Lucy.

"Up the top. You can see right over from there, down the combe and up the other side. That's where we might see something."

They left the bracken behind and walked over heather, thick and springy under their feet, bone-dry. The day had grown up a little, with a suggestion of an invisible sun risen somewhere behind the hills. It was quite still, without even a whisper of wind, and the air was clear and clean as stream water and the great shoulders of the moor bright with detail—white specks of sheep grazing, cattle, an occasional horse, birds flitting above the heather. And above all a great silence, broken only by the mew of a buzzard circling overhead, sheep calling, ravens croaking in a clump of trees somewhere below them. It was like being alone in the early morning of the world, very long ago.

A curlew bubbled, and then swung low over their heads, calling anxiously. "She's got chicks," said Kester. "She'll try to lead us off. They must be somewhere near." They trod cautiously. The bird sailed low, settling and then rising again, and finally came to rest at the top of the rise, her curved bill sharp against the horizon as she watched them. They left her behind, making for the higher ground.

As they reached the top a new landscape opened up on the other side. The hillside plunged sharply down into a deep combe, reaching up from the chequered vale into the heart of the moor, and beyond the diminishing hills rolled away towards the flat grey of the sea, glittering, streaked by the wind with patterns of light and dark.

"Let's stop," said Kester.

They sat on the heather.

"It's like a mattress," said Lucy. "I'd like to sleep on it."

A heron floated up from the trees below, sharp against the green, trailing long legs. Above, the buzzard mewed again, sailing the sky in great sweeps and curves.

"Where are the deer?" said Lucy.

"Don't be so impatient. They should be here somewhere—there's usually some. But you've got to look for them."

They sat, scanning the hillside, the sun faintly warm on their backs now. Kester searched the heather, yard by yard, his eyes screwed up, the soft light fringing his thin face.

"We're out of luck. I don't think there's any about."

"Never mind. It's nice up here anyway."

They lay back, cushioned in heather.

"D'you often come?"

"Quite often. I used to come with Jim and the others, but they fool about now, or they want to bring guns and blast off at everything that moves. I'd sooner be on my own."

"Why did you do that last night? Getting at them so they'd chase you."

Kester stiffened, looked away. "Why shouldn't I?"

"I didn't like it."

"Huh. Anything else you don't like? I mean, just let me know, won't you?"

Lucy continued rashly. "You went all funny when you

were watching them, I thought you were feeling sick or something. Were you?"

He turned on her, furious. "What are you getting at? There's nothing the matter with me. And if I want to take the mickey out of old Jim Thacker it's my business, isn't it?"

Lucy said in a small, cold voice, "There's no need to lose your temper." Far away, on the opposite hillside, ravens were croaking from a clump of trees.

There was a wall of silence between them, no longer companionable. Kester was tearing a sprig of heather to bits, scowling. He muttered something.

Lucy, from depths of misery and offence, said, "What do you mean—it was like there was something making you do it? That's daft."

He turned and glared at her, then got up. "I'm going. You'd better come if you don't want to get left. You'd get lost up here, you would."

She followed him through the heather, a hundred yards behind, and the morning disintegrated around them. Heat haze clamped down on the sharp detail of the hills and a car horn blared in the combe. Flies swarmed from the bracken, Lucy slapped her arms and legs, hot and irritable. They were following the sheep tracks with the bracken high around them—Kester was only just visible far ahead as a movement in the sea of green. She stumbled on, boiling with emotion and distress. Her shoe had rubbed a blister on her heel and she stopped to tie a handkerchief round it. When she stood up again Kester was no longer in sight. She stared round in dismay, and then saw the bracken sway only a few yards ahead.

He's come back for me. Well, all right, but I'm jolly well not going to be the first to say sorry.

She saw the antlers first, lifting above the bracken, and

then as she rounded a little twist in the sheep track the creature's head came into view, staring out at her only a few yards from the path as it scrambled to its feet, head flung back as it scented her, already turning to bound away. She had only time to think, startled and half-afraid, that it was much smaller than she had expected, before it was gone, leaping through the bracken and down towards the combe.

She wondered if Kester had seen it, and then remembered that she had lost sight of him. That movement had been the stag.

He's probably waiting for me where we left the bikes, at that gate where the lane starts. I must be almost there now.

After ten minutes' walking she had reached the brow of the hill, but the gate was not there. Bracken stretched all round. Her heart was beginning to thud now, and sweat trickled down her face. She struggled on, and presently found herself looking down the hill, but where she had expected the neat field-pattern to begin the moor stretched away in front of her, rolling down into a small, deep combe that looked quite unfamiliar.

She stopped, panting, tormented by flies, and stared round. There was a movement somewhere behind and her stomach lurched sickeningly.

Not a stag. Please not. Are they fierce? Those antlers— coming out of the bracken like that . . .

But it was a large bird, something like a pheasant, exploding from the ground and whirring away low over the hill.

She turned and took a different track, not down but leading out over the shoulder of the hill. The gate and the lane must surely be that way. She must somehow have turned off the original track when she lost sight of Kester.

She walked for another ten minutes or so, and then suddenly realized that she was stepping over a mossy log she had crossed once before. She had walked in a complete circle.

The sun was high in the sky. She was hot and her throat ached with thirst. The bracken stalks stung her legs like a thousand whips and both feet were blistered now. She felt trapped, as though she were being driven to circle this same spot for ever, and suddenly panic swept through her and she started to run blindly, sobbing to herself, tripping and stumbling on the dry ground.

And then, as she began to stagger a little from dizziness and despair, there was the gate in front of her, and the lane beyond, tipping away down the hill.

Kester's bike was gone. Her own lay where she had left it, half in the ditch. She sat down on the grass and took her shoes off to inspect the blisters, feeling unaccountably foolish, and glad that no one had witnessed her panic. There was a tiny stream by the lane, running down from the moor, and she washed her aching feet in it and had a drink. Then, rested, she set off on the long free-wheeling ride back to the village, the bike slipping and skidding on the loose shaly surface of the lane and the high sun very hot on the back of her head.

SIX

"I GOT LOST up on the moor this morning. It was frightening. I felt as though I was going round in circles."

Aunt Mabel, busy at her desk, said abstractedly, "The people here would say you'd been pixy-led."

Lucy frowned, a little disapproving. There was a suspicion of whimsy about the suggestion. Perhaps Aunt Mabel sensed her reaction, for she said, "Not cosy pixies from fairy stories. Malevolent creatures. Some people think it's a very old memory from ancient times when there were still Stone Age folk living up on moors and wild places."

"I think I just lost the way. It's not very difficult when it's all bracken and everything looks the same."

"And where was Kester all this time?"

"He went on back. We'd had an argument."

"Dear me," said Aunt Mabel, "I hope it's all cleared up now."

"No, I don't think it is."

"Oh, well, put it down to the weather. Everyone gets irritable in this heat."

"I wish they wouldn't do this Dance. I feel worried. As

though something was going to happen, and I don't really understand what."

"My dear child, you mustn't feel so personally involved in everything. You're here to enjoy yourself."

"I did see a stag," said Lucy, "after Kester had gone. It was funny—it wasn't a bit like I'd expected."

"They never are. They always seem smaller and wilder."

"Yes, that was it—wild. I felt as thought I oughtn't to be there."

The day wore on, the sun climbing in a sky of piercing blue. There was not a breath of wind; the air was like felt. Lucy sat on her wall for a while, refusing to admit to herself that she was hoping Kester would pass, and was finally driven to seek refuge in the cool of the cottage. She read, and stared into the garden, drowning in the heat, as the day dragged slowly past. When at last it was evening she went upstairs, washed, and changed her dress. Coming down, she stared hard at the picture. It was difficult to identify the moorland featured in it; it might have been anywhere. There was no particular reason to think that the rise of the hill behind that curious antlered horse looked like the hill she and Kester had climbed that morning.

She wandered through the village. It was cooler now. The heat-haze had lifted and the flowers in the cottage gardens glowed, luminous in the evening light. People stood at their gates and leaned over walls.

"Terrible hot day it's been, eh?"

"Yes, we could do with rain now."

"Best have it like this for the Fête, though."

She met Kester in the little lane past the church, face to face, so that although it was what she had been expecting she was nevertheless taken aback, and stood speechless. At last he said, off-hand, "You get back all right this morning?"

There was a suggestion of apology. Lucy, from some

deep-seated urge to punish herself, ignored it and said, "'Course I did. I'm not stupid. And I saw a stag."

"Lucky old you, then."

They looked past each other, affecting indifference, waiting. "Well, cheerio, then."

"Goodbye."

Turning round once in the middle of the village to look back she saw him leaning against the wall by the stream, talking to some boys, with a couple of girls hanging on the outskirts of the group. Their laughter floated after her and as she hurried away she had the feeling that it was directed against her. Filled with resentment, and near to tears, she almost ran back to the cottage.

She woke some time in the early reaches of the night. It was barely dark, as though the twilight of the interminable summer evening were already giving way to dawn, in some brief arctic midnight. The clock by her bed said nearly twelve. She got up and looked out of the window for a moment, and then crept out on the landing to get a glass of water from the bathroom. As she did so she looked down for a moment into the hall.

There were only three pairs of antlers on the wall. And from outside came a faint click, as though the garden gate were just closing.

It took her barely a couple of minutes to pull off her nightdress and put on a sweater and jeans. She padded down the stairs, carrying her shoes in her hand.

"I've got to find out where they go. Who takes them? I've got to know."

In the kitchen, Whitby lay on his side, fast asleep, wheezing gently.

Fat lot of good you are as a watch-dog.

The trees and hedges were blank against the sky, stiff

shapes larger than their daylight forms. The cottages gleamed a little in the light of the moon climbing behind the hill, a flat disc suspended just above the curve of the land. It was absolutely quiet: the remembered noise of dawn seemed unbelievable.

She left the gate open behind her and stole along the lane, keeping close to the hedge and stopping every minute or so to listen. Some instinct took her up the valley rather than down into the village, though every now and then she glanced back over her shoulder. She was extremely frightened.

A hundred yards or so up the lane there was a gate into the meadow by the stream where she had swum with Kester. She climbed up and sat on the top, listening, and staring across the grass. The only sound was the gentle rush of the water and occasional rustlings in the hedge, the stirrings of birds and small animals. At the far side of the field woodland sloped steeply up the hill and as her eyes grew more used to the darkness she picked out a bunch of cattle, quite motionless in a far corner.

It was not so much movement as the sense of being watched that made her swing round and look back up the lane.

There was a dog standing in the middle of the road, twenty yards or so away, watching her. It was black, high and thin, with a sharp pointed nose and prick ears, and as it moved its head slightly the moonlight caught its eyes and they were bright green, like emeralds.

Lucy made a noise in her throat between a scream and a gasp. She slid off the gate and began to run back down the lane, and as she did so she had a second's glimpse of antlers, raised above the hedge, moving, dark and forked against the sky.

* * *

In the morning the antlers were in place, as she had known they would be. It could have been a dream, except that her shoes were still damp with dew when she woke from a heavy, stunned sleep, with the sun already high and Aunt Mabel clattering in the kitchen below.

"Aunt Mabel, do stags come down into the combe?"

"You seem to be obsessed with the things, child. No, I don't think it's very likely. There aren't any on the hills immediately around here—you have to go further into the moor."

"Do you know if anyone in the village has a big black dog?" This almost in an undertone, as though she could hardly bring herself to say it.

"I really couldn't tell you, dear—it's not the sort of thing I notice. But I daresay. It seems quite probable."

She went up to the Norton-Smiths after breakfast, diffident and a little embarrassed, but the girls greeted her with their usual imperturbable absorption in their own affairs.

"Oh, hello, Lucy. You've come just at the right time. D'you mind helping us with this beastly sewing? We've got to alter four costumes because they don't fit people properly. I say, d'you realize it's only ten days till the Fête?"

It was some time before she was able to place her question, casually, not to arouse their interest.

"Does anyone in the village have a big black dog?"

"Oh, I don't know. I can't think of one. Why? I didn't know you were interested in dogs, Lucy?"

"I am quite. I saw one and just wondered what kind it was."

"Miss Laycock has," said Louise suddenly. "You know— the one that's some kind of mongrel. It's just a puppy really."

"Who's Miss Laycock?"

"Oh, she lives in that cottage half-way up the hill. She's got two or three dogs. Lucy, you are sewing funnily, if you don't mind me saying—your stitches are ever so big, you know."

Lucy said cautiously, "Do you think you could take me there. To see the dog?"

The girls stared. "I s'pose so," said Caroline. "I mean, we don't know her awfully well, but we do see her sometimes."

"Today?"

"You are odd, Lucy, honestly. I mean, you get these ideas about something and then nothing else matters. Does it have to be today?"

"Yes."

"Oh, all right," said Caroline with a sigh, "but this evening, then. It's too hot to trail up there now. Actually Mummy did say she was going to send her up some gooseberries some time. Oh, gosh, I suppose that means we'll have to pick them."

"I will."

"Oh, thanks, Lucy."

They picked gooseberries in the afternoon, tormented by heat and prickles. Caroline and Louise grumbled and collapsed periodically to lie panting under an apple tree. Lucy worked on, sweat trickling down her face and neck. At least it was something to do and brought the evening closer. Mrs. Norton-Smith visited them once.

"Hello there, Lucy! Don't let me interrupt you—just carry on with the good work. I say, you're looking a bit peaky, my dear. Are you feeling under the weather?"

"No. Not really. Just a bit hot."

Mrs. Norton-Smith gave her a curious glance and went away.

After tea they climbed the hill to Miss Laycock's cottage. It was a small pink-washed building set up on the hillside away from the village, seeming to grow out of the tiny garden that sloped steeply up behind it and fell away in front. As Caroline pushed open the gate several dogs exploded barking from various directions. Miss Laycock came out, exhorting them to be quiet. Caroline presented the gooseberries and introduced Lucy, who was staring round distractedly. The only dogs to appear had been two small terriers and an alsatian. They stood around for a few moments, and then Caroline said, "I think we'd better be getting back."

Lucy moved closer and kicked her on the ankle.

"Ouch! Oh, Miss Laycock, Lucy wondered if she could see your other dog. The black one."

"Sheba?" said the woman, a little surprised, "yes, I daresay she's around somewhere. Are you interested in dogs, then?"

"Yes," said Lucy, flushing.

Miss Laycock whistled. The dog appeared from somewhere behind the cottage. It was black, with pointed nose and prick ears, and a thick busy tail tipped with white, that swept to and fro deprecatingly as it approached them. Its eyes were a soft brown, and the prick ears flattened as it pushed its muzzle lovingly into Miss Laycock's hand. Lucy made a movement and it sprang back in alarm, the tail sinking between its legs.

"Frightfully nervous dog," said Miss Laycock. "There, Sheba, don't be silly. They're not going to hurt you."

"We must go," said Caroline, "Mummy'll be wondering."

As they walked away Lucy looked back once. The dog was standing at the gate, and as she stared at it again she realized that she would never know for sure if it was the dog she had seen last night or not.

A hot wind had risen, gusting down the village street and swirling the iced-lolly papers and cigarette cartons in the gutter. The sky was streaked with drifts of thin white cloud, but the sun still burned their bare arms and legs.

"We are lucky," said Caroline, "having such a lovely summer."

Lucy slapped a horse-fly on her neck and turned her head aside as they passed the barely identifiable remains of some small animal, pasted on the road by car-tyres.

Outside the forge, the smith was leaning against the wall, smoking a pipe and talking to another man. Lucy hung back a little, her heart beating fast.

"Come on, Lucy."

"You go on. I'm not going back yet."

"Oh, all right, then."

"And thank you, Caroline. About the dog, I mean."

She stopped, pretending to tie a shoe-lace. The men were still talking. At last one moved away.

"Well, cheerio, then, Tom."

"Cheerio, Bill."

Lucy straightened up. There was no one else in earshot now. The smith had been watching her all the time.

"You looking for young Kester?"

"No."

There was a silence. The smith puffed at his pipe, the smoke streaming away in the wind.

Lucy said, "Please, Mr. Hancock, could you tell me something?"

"Eh?"

"The Hunt—the Wild Hunt. What would happen to a person if—if they actually saw it?"

"I thought you were like Kester. Reckoned it were a lot o' rubbish."

She said in a low voice, "I'm not all that sure now. Anyway, that was Kester, not me."

"Huh."

"Please. Why don't people want to see them?"

He looked at her as though the question were unnecessary, and then said, "Because once you seen them you're a part of them, aren't you, girl? You're with them under the same sky and treading the same ground. And they're a Hunt, aren't they? They have to hunt something, or someone, don't they?"

SEVEN

SHE MET KESTER several times during the next few days. Twice he was alone, and they pretended not to see each other. Afterwards, Lucy went home and dug furiously in Aunt Mabel's vegetable garden, tearing out the spent stems of broad-bean plants and stabbing the fork down into the hard soil. On another occasion he did not see her: he was outside the village hall, leaning on his bike, carrying on a shouted conversation with Jim Thacker and a bunch of the other boys, all of them, Lucy noticed, members of the Dance. She listened, lurking in the shelter of the garage wall.

"How's the dancing-class coming on, then? Nicely on our toes, are we, in time with the music?" Kester, grinning broadly, was poised for flight should it be necessary.

"Shut up, you."

"Hobby-horse not giving trouble again, I hope?"

"You watch it, Kester Lang. We'll get you, you know. It won't be long now."

"Just try," said Kester. "You just try. We'll see who's fastest."

"We're biding our time."

"I can wait."

"There's more of us. You're on your own, you are."

Kester jumped on the bike and rode away, laughing.

The garage man, stooped over a car engine, looked after him and said to the postman, "I reckon that boy's looking for trouble."

"He's a queer lad. Not like t'others round here."

Walking past the pub, she noticed someone sweeping up broken glass in the yard. There was a police car parked outside. In the shop, the women were talking in low voices.

"What come over young Fletcher in the "Arms" last night, then?"

"They say it were Bill went for 'ee first, and then fists come out all round."

"Police aren't bringing no charges, though. So long as it don't happen again."

"We never had fightin' here before."

"It's this weather. It do make everyone terrible bad tempered."

It was true. Even Aunt Mabel had spoken curtly that morning.

Lucy took to spending time at the Norton-Smiths. There was something almost soothing about Caroline and Louise. They were so equable, so unaware of almost everything, that being with them was like being alone. They occupied themselves with their own affairs, chiefly the interminable business of tending the ponies, and Lucy sat in the shade, staring unseeing into the heat haze, and brooding. Once she wandered into the house and stood in the carpeted hall, listening to the ticking of a clock somewhere in the silence. There was a smell of polish. In a corner the Dancers' antlers were stacked carelessly against the wall. She went over and touched them: they were cool and smooth, like ivory, the masks below clumsily cut from leather, the eye sockets a little jagged round the edges where the scissors had torn them. She lifted one and held it for a moment against her head, and then put it down again quickly.

A door opened somewhere and Mrs. Norton-Smith came hurrying down a passage and into the hall.

"Oh, Lucy, it's you . . . I thought it was the Vicar. He's supposed to be coming up to discuss some Fête business." She turned to go into the kitchen.

Lucy said in a strangled voice, "Mrs. Norton-Smith . . ."

"Yes, Lucy?"

"I know it's none of my business, but I wish you—they—wouldn't do this Dance."

"My dear child, why ever not?"

Lucy was scarlet in the face, slightly dizzy. "I don't know. I can't explain. I just feel it shouldn't be done. I'm sorry . . ."

Mrs. Norton-Smith looked quite concerned. "Are you sure you're feeling all right these days, my dear? I didn't like to mention it but I have thought you've been looking a bit off-colour. I wonder if I should pop along and have a word with your aunt?"

"No, thank you," said Lucy, "I'm quite all right. It doesn't matter."

"Not homesick or anything? Enjoying the holidays?"

Lucy nodded, mutely. Mrs. Norton-Smith patted her on the shoulder and said, "Well then, snap out of it, there's a good girl. Get these funny ideas out of your head, eh?"

The Vicar appeared at the open door.

"Ah, there you are, Vicar. I was just beginning to wonder if you'd forgotten."

"I'm sorry to be late. A bit of trouble over this business in the pub last night, you know. The police wanted a word. However I think it's all sorted out. No repercussions, I hope.

People seem to behave a bit out of character in this heat."

"Jolly good," said Mrs. Norton-Smith vaguely. "Now come along. We've got to sort out this business of the programme." They walked away down the passage, talking. Lucy went out into the garden again to go back to the stables. As she passed by the house Mrs. Norton-Smith's voice came through an open window.

". . . really the most odd child. Not a bit like one's own girls. There's something there you feel you can't quite handle. Personally I prefer children to be quite straightforward, if you see what I mean." Lucy hurried away, shoulders hunched and cheeks burning.

Later, she sat at the table in her bedroom, staring at the lump of pink alabaster. It had been lying in the sun on the window-sill and was warm, like something live. The ammonite was in her top drawer, wrapped in a clean handkerchief.

She took a sheet of paper and began to write a letter to her father.

. . . I am very well but it is too hot. Aunt Mabel sends her love. Caroline and Louise's mother's horse had a dead foal and she got all upset, not that she seems the sort of person who gets upset. I went up on the moor with Kester at dawn and it was lovely but then I saw a stag and got lost. I got back in the end. I haven't seen Kester for a few days now. That Dance they are doing that I told you about is quite soon now. At the beginning Kester and I laughed at them but now I think it is creepy. They are hoping it will make a lot of money for the church roof, but I hope it will rain because it is too hot and it makes everyone bad tempered. I will tell you if I see Kester again.

Love from Lucy.

She was putting the letter into the envelope when a movement in the lane beyond the window attracted her attention. Heads, bobbing above the wall: first Jim Thacker's ginger crop of hair, and then the other boy Dancers. They were walking in silence, one behind the other, without their usual shouts and scuffles, and they carried the garish bundles of their costumes slung over their shoulders, and the antlers. Lucy stared. That they should have the costumes was not in itself remarkable: perhaps they were on their way to a rehearsal of the Dance. But the Dance rehearsals always took place in the evening. And the Vicar had gone off somewhere in his car—it had passed only a few minutes before. She watched, puzzled, as they went by. Then she got up and went out into the garden and down the path to the gate. The boys were still in sight, going past the pub. Lucy felt suddenly convinced that whatever they were about to do involved Kester. And yet he had not been with them. She began to follow them up the lane, keeping in the shelter of the hedge.

As she passed the pub a movement in the shadowed yard made her jump. The smith had stepped forward, a mug of beer in his hand. He was staring up the lane, where the boys were just visible climbing over a gate into a field. Lucy tried to pass unobserved but he saw her and said, "I'd leave them be if I was you."

She said, trying to sound unconcerned, "I'm just going for a walk."

The big man seemed curiously disturbed. He shifted his mug from hand to hand and then said, "That Vicar's a fool. He don't know what he's at."

"What?" said Lucy uneasily.

"Have you seen young Kester?"

"No."

"He'd do best to steer clear o' they lads."

"Why? They wouldn't really do anything to him, would they? It's just a game, isn't it?"

"It were. It were. But there's no knowing, now. Not with the Dance come back. I tell you, they don't know what they're at. Her up there and that Vicar."

Lucy glanced up the lane again. The boys were out of sight now. She still felt compelled to follow them, but there was another question she had to ask. She said, "Mr. Hancock, it is just a Dance, isn't it? I mean, it seems so creepy sometimes. There's—there's nothing more to it, is there?"

The pub door opened. There was a clink of glasses and a sour, beery smell. Two men came out.

"Mornin', Tom."

"Mornin', Leslie." The smith turned away from Lucy. She said, "Mr. Hancock..." But he was already moving towards the open door, his glass empty, saying something to one of the other men. As he reached the door he seemed to remember her, and called out, "If you see young Kester, tell him he's wanted back home."

Lucy nodded. Then she walked quickly away up the lane, keeping in the shadow of the hedge. The sun was high in the sky, the heat thumping down on to the countryside and quivering in the air above the lane. It was very still. In the corners of fields, cattle were bunched in black pools of shade, flicking their tails against the flies. The hedgerows were silent and lifeless, except that a bush that had seemed studded all over with brown fruit stirred as she approached and lifted into the air as a cloud of small birds. Warm, gusting smells almost stifled her—manure, cow, and the rotting scent of meadowsweet.

The gate over which the boys had vanished was the one which led into the big field with the stream and as she climbed over it she could see them in the distance wading through the water, the clothes and antlers lifted above their heads. Were they going swimming? But they never swam without an accompaniment of screams and horse-play: now they were silent, purposeful. And in any case they were leaving the water, crossing the field the other side and vanishing into a small copse beyond. Lucy jumped down from the gate and began to run along the track down to the stream, at once curious and strangely apprehensive. It seemed suddenly very important not to lose sight of them.

In the copse she was filled with alarm. She could no longer hear or see them. Was it a trick? Were they lying in wait for someone? Kester? Herself, even? But they had never taken any notice of her, ignoring her totally: as a girl, and a stranger at that, she interested them not at all. In any case, they could not possibly know she would follow them. She crept forward, her heart thumping a little louder than usual, listening and searching the undergrowth for movement.

And then, a little muffled by the bushes but none the less clearly audible, there came a strange sound. A squeak, a rattle, a sobbing whine that sent a blackbird shrieking from the brambles and stopped Lucy in her tracks with a little gasp. It was the music of the Dance: the flute, the strings, the drum thumping dully in the still silence of the midday heat.

She moved as quietly as she could to the edge of the copse, and peered out through the trees. There was a water-meadow on the other side, darkly green and sparkling with buttercups, shaded by the band of woodland spilling down from the steep hillside which overhung it. The stream ran through the middle, deep and sluggish at this point. Lucy stared in amazement. The Dancers were moving silently, the noise of their feet mopped up by the lush grass so that they seemed dream-like—queer, bright figures moving to and fro in the formal patterns of the Dance, bobbing to one another, winding snake-like for a minute, and then breaking up again, with only the music wailing in the quietness of the valley. None of the girl Dancers were present. The six boys held the masks and antlers lifted in front of them, so that the shadows pranced blackly on the grass alongside, but as they turned level with Lucy she caught a glimpse of their faces, rapt, expressionless, almost unrecognizable.

She leaned forward to get a better view, and suddenly the dead branch under her hand snapped with a loud, dry noise. The Dancers swung round towards her, their eyes glaring through the leather sockets and as she jumped hurriedly backwards into the copse they began to move across the grass towards her. She heard Jim Thacker's voice, thick and distorted, say, "Who's there? Who were that? Get after 'im!" and as she turned to run she heard them crashing behind her.

She began to run through the trees, deeper into the woodland, climbing the side of the hill, through the green half-light sliced by the dark poles of tree-trunks. She could hear the boys somewhere behind, scrambling through the bracken and brambles. They were no longer shouting, but the noise of their heavy breathing came to her from close behind, and she found herself fleeing in a kind of panic up the hillside, sweat streaming down her face, her breath coming in short gasps. Her flight had been instinctive: it was not until she was almost at the top of the hill, with the trees thinning out and the open, bracken-covered common visible beyond, that her panic began to recede a little, and reason took over.

Why run away, in any case? They can't do anything to me—they're only a lot of boys. It was just that it was all so creepy, them dancing all by themselves like that, and looking at me through the masks when they heard me. Did they think I was Kester?

She stopped, and turned round. They were coming up

the hill behind her, spread out among the trees. Rather breathlessly, she called out, "Look, stop it. You gave me a fright, that's all. I didn't mean anything . . ."

She took a step forward to meet them, as they came pounding up through the trees. Suddenly she could see their faces—Jim Thacker's, and the Fool, and the rest of them. Their eyes were bulging, with the same glassy look she had noticed when they were dancing, but now there was something else there that made her stomach twist. A kind of madness: an obsession.

Lucy said again, "Please stop . . . ," but they seemed not to hear as they came stumbling on towards her. It was almost as though they did not see her, either. And then Jim Thacker shouted again in the same thickened voice, "There! Get after 'im!" and she turned and fled away into the bracken, still crying, "Look, stop it, will you . . . Don't be daft . . ." But she knew now they were not listening.

She ploughed through the bracken, tripping against hidden molehills and rabbit burrows, and then all of a sudden she was brought to a sudden stop, confronted with a high wire fence running along in front of her in both directions. The deer fence along the top of the hill . . . She tore frantically beside it for a short distance, like a caged animal, and then remembered that the nearest gate was down in the combe, at least half a mile away. She swerved back into the bracken and began to plunge down the hill again, back into the woods, and she heard the Dancers close in behind her.

Down through the trees again, a slipping, sliding, panicky progress, clutching her side, where cramp stabbed at her, seeing through a mist of sweat the beads of blood on her arms where brambles had torn the skin. And all the time the horrid noise of those crashing feet behind. She began to sob, in sharp, dry gasps.

She reached the bottom, and turned left along the track that led into the water meadow. The trees ended suddenly and she could see the stream ahead, and the pool where she had swum with Kester. Completely exposed now, she ran out on to the grass, and beside her flowed the stream, green and sluggish, weed streaming just under the surface, glutinous bubbles floating on the top. The cries of the boys sounded like the baying of hounds behind.

"There 'e goes! We'll get 'im now!"

"Give 'im a ducking, shall we?"

They were close behind. Hopelessly, she made for the feeble shelter of a willow spreading its branches over the water. She had no breath: she could run no further. As they came up on her she was half collapsed against the tree, her heart thudding and everything spinning in front of her eyes. She could barely see their faces, peering down at her as they closed in, standing over her in a half-circle.

And then the mists cleared, and the spinning stopped, and she looked at them. They were red with sun and exertion, their hair streaked across glistening foreheads, but their eyes were no longer staring. They looked dazed, puzzled. One of them said, "It's that girl. Miss Clough's niece. Friend o' Kester's," and looked away in embarrassment.

Jim Thacker said awkwardly "'Ere, you all right?" and stretched out a hand to help her up. Lucy pushed him away angrily and stood up, brushing leaves and dust from her clothes.

One of the boys said in a low voice, "How'd we get here? I thought we was doing the Dance? Practising, like." They looked at Lucy, and at one another, blinking.

Lucy said coldly, "You chased me, if you want to know. All up the hill and then down here."

They were silent, shuffling and looking away. Lucy said, "Did you think I was Kester?"

They stared. One of them said, "Kester Lang? What's 'e got to do with it?" There was real bewilderment in their faces: they began to back away from her. Jim Thacker said, "Sorry. We didn't mean it. It were an accident, like."

Lucy glared. She smoothed her hair back, snatched the ribbon that one of the boys had picked up and was handing to her, and began to walk away down the path towards the village. Once she turned to look back at them. They were wandering away back to the water-meadow, hands thrust in pockets, talking in low voices. She heard Jim Thacker say "Where'd she come from, then? I don't remember seein' her come. Hope she won't start no trouble." Someone else mumbled a reply, inaudible, and Lucy hurried away, red and angry. The sun beat down on her head, almost unbearably hot.

Kester came to the cottage that evening, curious, and indignant. "What's it all about? What d'you want to get mixed up with Jim Thacker and that lot for?"

"It wasn't my fault," said Lucy. "They all started chasing me. It was beastly, I can tell you." She did not mention the Dance.

"You must have set them off somehow. Said something."

"I didn't."

"Well, why bring me into it? Bill Fowler said you started saying did they think you were me or something."

Lucy flushed. "What else did they say?"

"Well, nothing, really. I only found out by accident, and then Bill told me, when I said I'd tell who pinched the Vicar's apples otherwise. He didn't want to. What's up?"

"I don't know," said Lucy, near to tears. "You should, though."

"What d'you mean? I still don't get why you were mixed up with them. Why run away in the first place?"

"I had to," said Lucy, "it was like in the Dance. They were all the Dancers, you see."

"Well, what's that got to do with it? No one gets chased in the Dance."

"That's what *you* think."

"What on earth do you mean?"

"I don't know. At least I'm not sure."

"Well, stop talking daft, then," said Kester angrily; "and don't get mixed up with that lot. You made me look a fool, apart from anything else. Talking about me like that."

"Well, don't *you* get mixed up with them either. You've been asking for trouble. Making fun of them over the Dance and everything."

"Look, that's my business, what I get up to. It's different for me. I'm just having a bit of fun. What could they do to me, anyway?"

They glared at each other in the cool of Aunt Mabel's sitting-room. Lucy could feel tears pricking behind her eyes.

"I wish you wouldn't, Kester."

"So you keep saying."

"Something'll happen. And you know, too, don't you? I know you do, because of that time with your uncle, when he was talking to you. When he said, 'There'll be hunting this summer.'" She stared accusingly at him.

"Look, just forget my uncle. He talks a load of rubbish most of the time."

"But it meant something when he said that. I know—I saw your face."

"I was just having him on. And you."

"You weren't. You were scared."

"Scared! Don't make me laugh! Anyway, what's it to do with the Dance? That was before all this Dance business began. Remember?" He grinned triumphantly, inviting her to contradict.

"It's all mixed up," said Lucy.

"You mean *you're* all mixed up."

There was silence for a moment. The dog came into the room, looked at them, and went out again, his claws clicking on the floor-boards.

Kester said suddenly, "Anyway, suppose I want to know what it's all about? S'pose I *want* it to happen? Or suppose it has to happen?" This last in a different voice, quiet, almost remote.

"That means you believe it then. There is something."

"I didn't say that."

"But you think there might be."

"It's like that shape in the cliff," said Kester. "Was it a dinosaur or wasn't it? You can't ever be quite sure."

"I'd rather not find out."

"Well, that's you. I'm different. I've got to know."

"Even though you're scared stiff?"

For a minute he looked as though he might hit her. He went very red, his mouth thin and white. But he said nothing and after a moment he turned and went quickly out of the cottage.

Aunt Mabel came in through the open garden door.

"Dear, dear. Was that Kester? I thought I heard voices raised in anger."

"We were arguing," said Lucy sullenly.

Aunt Mabel gave her a sharp look. "You two were such friends, I thought. What's happened?"

"Nothing. It's not important."

"Just as you like, my dear. Anyway, it's not for me to interfere. But it seems a pity. Dear me, when will the rain come? My garden is expiring for lack of water. I've never known such a month."

After supper they walked together through the village. The combe was filled with a pearly light, the trees black and dusty, the cottage walls bright ochre when the dying sun touched them. It was still very warm.

As they passed the village hall the whine and thump of music could be heard from the recreation ground on the other side. Aunt Mabel stopped. "They must be rehearsing this Dance of theirs. Shall we have a look?"

Lucy said nothing, and followed her aunt reluctantly.

The Dance had progressed considerably. The musicians had achieved some kind of unity, an insistent rhythm rather than a melody, to which the twelve Dancers matched their prancing steps, their strange figures swaying to and fro against the bright grass, with the dark cliff of trees rising beyond them. The antlers lifted above their heads, dark forked shapes throwing shadows that leaped and flickered behind the Dancers. Caroline and the other girls occasionally spoke or giggled, but the boys were silent and absorbed, moving as though in a trance. They breathed heavily, and their faces behind the masks were set and stolid.

"Good gracious!" said Aunt Mabel. "What a curious performance. Really most odd!"

The Vicar came up to them. "Good morning, Miss Clough. Come to inspect our little effort? What do you think of it?"

"Very interesting," said Aunt Mabel politely.

"I'm glad to say we seem to have ironed out our teething troubles. Between you and me we had rather a lot of bother with some of the village lads to begin with. Fooling about, you know—hooliganism. But they seem to be taking it quite seriously now, indeed they've become quite curiously involved in it. I've really been rather surprised myself."

The Dancers stamped and shuffled, forming a line that curled back on itself. The Fool's bells rang out in the still evening.

"Yes, it's very odd," the Vicar went on. "They're quite intense about it. Mind, I've had some different reactions among the older people. One or two of the elderly women have asked me to put a stop to it. Isn't that curious? But of course that would be out of the question, when the youngsters are having such fun. And there's no doubt it's going to be a considerable tourist attraction for the Fête."

"Quite," said Aunt Mabel. "Tell me, do you know the full history of this Dance? I gather it's an ancient survival of some kind."

"No, we don't, I'm afraid. Just how many Dancers there were, and what they were, from the church records."

"You don't know why it was done?"

"No idea," said the Vicar. "Interesting, aren't they, these old customs? Excuse me a moment, I must tell the Manwoman to leave a wider gap." He hurried away, shouting instructions.

A few minutes later the Dancers broke up, peeling off their costumes and throwing down the antlers. The boys went off together in a group, laughing and joking, discarding their former intensity with the costumes. Jim Thacker caught sight of Lucy and looked away again at once in obvious embarrassment. Caroline came up to them, pink-faced, sweat glistening on her forehead.

"Honestly, you get so hot doing this, and the Vicar makes us work so hard. I think I'm going to collapse. Come back with us and have a freezing cold drink, Lucy."

"Go on if you'd like to, dear," said Aunt Mabel. "I have to call on someone for a few minutes anyway."

Caroline and Lucy walked slowly back up the lane.

"Actually, it's really coming on quite well. The Dance, I mean. Those boys don't mess about any more. Not long now till the day."

They passed the smith sitting on the wall outside the forge. Caroline said "Good evening" brightly, but he paid no attention to her. Looking hard at Lucy, he said, "I hear you had some trouble today."

"It was nothing. It didn't matter."

"Did they think you was someone else?"

Lucy was silent.

"I reckon it's bound to come now, you know, girl."

They walked on. "What on earth was that about?" said Caroline.

"Never mind. Nothing."

EIGHT

THE CLOUDLESS DAYS unfurled, one after another, progressing from dewy mornings through the pulsing heat of the day to soft, luminous evenings. Already in mid-August the harvesters had begun their slow crawling in the fields, yellow monsters carving wide paths through the barley. The stubble blossomed into creeping lines of flame as the straw was burnt off, leaving tiger-stripes of black and gold curving over the hillsides. Blackberries ripened, house-martins gathered on the telephone lines, and here and there a sharp blaze of gold among the trees was a reminder that it would be autumn before long. But still it did not rain: the countryside lay slack in the heat, waiting, the dark shapes of trees and hedges still and misty.

Lucy would lie awake at night, staring at the ceiling, a victim of every noise beyond her window, the creeping, rustling, pattering activities of the darkness.

And the Fête, which had been merely a date in the calendar, became actual as preparations began. In the recreation field, marquees were going up, a tangle of ropes and pegs, labelled "Refreshments," "Flower Tent" and "Dog Show."

"Though if this super weather goes on we could have had the whole lot in the open," said Mrs. Norton Smith. "Not like last year, with duck-boards and straw down everywhere."

"I hear Combe St. Margaret aren't doing at all well with their Appeal," said the Vicar. "They've not even reached half the target yet. We must pray for a bit of divine favouritism," he added, with an amiable chuckle.

Mrs. Norton-Smith turned away pointedly: "I never think that sort of joke is in frightfully good taste, coming from a clergyman," she said.

"Mummy!" said Caroline in an undertone, "I think he heard." But Mrs. Norton-Smith was already on her way to issue instructions to the workmen struggling with the marquees.

Lucy drifted about the village, a restless observer, trailing from one place to another, always alert for a glimpse of Kester. And when, accidentally, they did approach one another, the same ritual repeated itself—the agonized hope that he would make the first move, the obstinate refusal to look towards him, and the stomach-sinking moment as he passed her by, whistling, staring deliberately away.

"Have you gone off Kester or something?" said Caroline.

Lucy said, "I suppose so," and then loathed herself for her betrayal.

"Those boys were after him yesterday evening," said Louise. "Jim Thacker and the others. They tried to take his bike and throw it in the stream, but he got away."

Lucy froze, saying nothing.

"Jim Thacker's rather a rough boy."

"Actually, Caro, he's doing awfully well at the Dance now—haven't you noticed? And the others too."

"Yes, I know. It's peculiar, really. They get quite different when they're doing it, almost as though they were somebody else. Sort of dreamy. Their eyes go all funny."

"Yes, I've noticed that too. What's the matter, Lucy, where are you going...? Honestly Lucy is *odd* the way she suddenly walks off for no reason at all."

"Aunt Mabel, do you know why they did this Dance thing in the old days?"

"Oh, I imagine it was some kind of fertility rite. To get the crops to grow, you know, or to encourage the sun to rise again after the winter."

"Just that? Nothing else?"

"My dear child, I'm not a walking encyclopaedia. Ask Mr. Hancock at the forge. He's a mine of traditional information, I'm told."

"No, I don't think I will, thank you."

And every evening, in the darkening field, the antlers were lifted again to the sky, under the dying sun, and the twelve figures leaped and capered on the grass, as the whine and jangle of an old music sang in the stillness of the valley.

Even Aunt Mabel was drawn into the general activity.

"I'm a poor, weak creature. I must have been out of my mind, letting Mrs. Turnbull talk me into saying I'd give ten pounds of plum jam for her stall. *And* arrange a display of wild flowers. You'll have to help me, Lucy."

The plums were hardly a problem: just a lengthy task of picking, stoning and stirring. The flowers were different.

"What on earth are we to find in the middle of August? With the hedges already cut."

"Couldn't we use berries too, Aunt Mabel? And toadstools and things from the wood. All labelled with Latin names."

"Bright child! Yes, why not. We'll go on a search tomorrow. Unless you've got anything planned with Kester."

"No. No, I haven't."

Lucy, tired after a long day in the sun, wandering aimlessly round the village, and a late evening helping Aunt Mabel with the jam, had slept more soundly than usual. Only once she had woken with a jump to hear Whitby barking in the kitchen below. Aunt Mabel's door had opened and she fell asleep again almost at once as she heard her aunt clumping down the stairs to quieten the dog.

They set off after breakfast, carrying baskets.

"Look at that!" said Aunt Mabel irritably, tapping a rose-bush with her stick, "a whole shoot snapped right off. And another one there. There's been a cow or something in the garden. Really, it's too bad." Whitby was sniffing at the ground, growling, the hairs on his back standing up in a dark ridge.

They walked through the village. It was early yet, with few people around, though here and there an old man or woman stood at a cottage gate, blinking in the bright sunshine.

"Good morning, Mrs. Taylor."

"Morning, Miss Clough. It were a bad night again. Noisy."

"I don't know about that," said Aunt Mabel vaguely. Her glance fell on a freshly-dug bed, planted with young cabbages. "I see you've had unwelcome visitors too." The bed was pitted with the prints of animal feet.

"That's so. They come right down through the village last night, and up over the hill."

"Wretched nuisance. People should be more careful not to let their creatures stray."

"There's nothing to be done. Best not to look nor listen."

"Nonsense. One must complain to the farmer concerned."

The old woman stared for a moment uncomprehendingly,

and then turned to look away towards the sky above the hills, hung with piles of bright cloud.

They left the village and began to follow the lane up the hill, searching the hedgerows as they went.

"Ah! Some bladder campion. And here's sheepsbit, and self-heal, and plenty of ground ivy. There's more survived the depredations of the County Council than one might imagine."

"What about these berries, Aunt Mabel?"

"Woody nightshade. Poisonous, but decorative. Take some but don't put your fingers in your mouth afterwards. Let us head for the wood and see if we can find some spurge, and some of the fungoids, and we might look by the stream on the way for the marshy things."

Fresh tongues of fern and bracken had sprung from the newly-trimmed banks of the lane, cool green fans against the fading grass and leaves. The earth, after weeks of drought, was a powdery pink, a fine dust on the surface of the lane. Lucy wandered behind her aunt, occasionally reaching into the mossy depths of the bank for a flower or berry. This was the lane she and Kester had spun down so often on their bicycles: she knew every twist, every gateway, every tree. They turned into a field, following the track that led down to the stream, but the barley that had shivered in the wind like stiff horsetails was cut now and the field prickly with stubble, dotted with square bales of straw. Already, down by the stream, a tractor was ploughing it up: the freshly-turned earth was a vivid ochre against the pale stubble. Gulls floated behind the tractor like shreds of paper.

"I do believe there are some kingcups still out," said Aunt Mabel, "under the bank there. Go and have a look for me, there's a good girl."

Lucy ran ahead towards the stream, her eyes on the gleam of yellow against the bank on the far side. To reach it she had to leave the path and cross the ploughed strip, her feet sinking deeply into the soft earth. When she had picked the flowers she turned to go back the way she had come and saw what she had failed to notice before. Her own footprints on the bare soil were surrounded by a confusion of other marks—the deep, curved prints of hoof-marks and the light dabs of dogs' paws, many of them, criss-crossing and overlapping each other, leading up from the stream and over the plough until they vanished into the stubble.

She stood staring at the marks, and the sound of her own heart thumping was loud in her ears.

When Aunt Mabel came over the field to join her she pointed at the ground, and said, in a half-whisper, "Look!"

"What, dear? Oh, the hounds have been out, I should imagine."

"I thought you said there wasn't any hunting in the summer."

"They still have to be exercised. One sees them around from time to time. Early in the morning usually."

"Oh. Oh, I see."

They crossed the stream and followed the path up into the wood. Sunlight crackled down through the branches, a rabbit skittered in the undergrowth, overhead wood-pigeons crashed awkwardly from tree to tree. Lucy hunted in the boles of trees for toadstools, lurid yellows and scarlets, her mind elsewhere. Finally Aunt Mabel was satisfied with their collection and they made their way back to the village through the fields and over the top of the hill.

As they passed the forge the smith came out and stood watching them, muscular arms crossed on his chest.

"Morning, Miss Clough."

"Morning to you, Mr. Hancock. You know my niece, Lucy, I think?"

"I do that. Reckon she's just about one of us now."

Aunt Mabel had moved on down the street. Lucy hung back for a moment, despite herself, sliding glances towards Kester's cottage.

The smith said, "Looking for Kester? He were here, not long since. Coming and going all the time, he is, like a cat on hot bricks. Poking fun at the other lads. Asking for trouble."

"It's not his fault he doesn't fit in with them. It's just that he's growing up different."

"There's no call for him to set himself apart, is there?" the man snapped, a real harshness in his voice, and Lucy's cheeks flamed.

"He hasn't. It's just happened."

The smith grunted, and turned to go into the forge. Lucy said, "I'm sorry. I know it's not my business."

"That's all right, girl. You mean well, I know that."

On a sudden impulse, Lucy said, "Can I come and watch you?"

"You're welcome. Mind the old mare, though. She's got a nasty temper."

There was a cart-horse tethered to the wall of the forge, an immense bulk looming up in the shadows. Lucy stared at the huge muscles sliding under its skin as it shifted restlessly, and the silky hair flowing over great feet.

"Gosh, I've never seen one of those! I thought nobody used them any more."

"They don't. She don't work no more, this old girl. They brings her out for shows, like. That's why she's to be shod— for the County Show next week."

The horse laid her ears back, rolling her eyes and clattering her hooves on the cobbles as the man approached her.

"Steady now, girl, steady. Mind, they did a good job on these hills, in the old days, the work-horses. A horse and plough won't tip over and pin a man down on a steep-pitched field like a tractor will. When I were a boy all the farmers round here had a couple of horses on the place, or more. Now there's none."

Lucy said, "I s'pose that means not so much work for you. Shoeing."

The smith was hissing between his teeth as his file grated against the horse's hoof. "This is the only forge left for ten miles round, where once there were one in every village."

Lucy pushed the hair out of her eyes, peering at him through the gloom, and said cautiously, "Then wouldn't Kester do better if he did some other kind of job. I mean, if there's fewer and fewer horses..."

He dropped the horse's hoof and snapped, with a sudden flare of temper, "We've always kept the forge, in my family. For hundreds of years. It's right Kester should do it, as I've no boy of my own." The fire rose, and roared, as he set the bellows going.

Lucy was silent. She picked up an unshaped shoe from a heap on the bench, feeling the cold of the iron against her hand and running her fingers over the grainy metal. The smith held another in his pincers: as the fire grew it began to glow, and became incandescent, thick and light. On the anvil, it twisted and spread under the hammer.

"You wouldn't think it could do that," said Lucy; "get all bendy like that. Not looking at it when it's cold."

"Aye, it's fine stuff, iron, fine stuff. It'll shoe your horse, and bind your wheel, and I don't know what else besides."

"Swords in the old days," said Lucy.

"That's so. It's no wonder folk have always thought a lot of it. You'll find many houses still like to have a bit of iron by, even nowadays, over the door, or by the hearth."

"Why?"

"For its power, girl, for its power."

There was a noise from the lane outside: hooves ringing on the tarmac and a man's voice shouting harshly. The smith straightened and set down the hammer and shoe.

"Hounds must be out. I can hear 'em." He moved towards the door and Lucy followed him. They stood looking down the lane.

The hounds filled the road, a seething, amiable horde of waving tails and lolling tongues, bright black, white and tan coats against the grey of the road, stopping to forage in a ditch, investigate a garden fence, dart up a cottage path. They surged around Lucy and Mr. Hancock. She felt a great head thrust against her hand, a leathery tongue rasping her bare leg, warm bodies pressing up to her, and then a whip snapped again as a man on a horse clattered by shouting at the dogs, and they moved away, their paws padding softly on the road. She looked up, and saw two red-faced men on big, heavy horses bawling, cracking whips. The long snake-like thongs licked among the dogs, sending them cantering on up the road, the coarse shouts of the men tore the still air and brought people to their doors. Only the hounds were quiet, loping past. "Twenty couple," said Mr. Hancock, "that'll be the young 'uns."

Lucy stared after them. She thought of the stag she had seen, small, brown and wild in the bracken. And yet, strangely, it was not the dogs that disturbed her but the men. Their hard faces and rough voices stayed with her for several minutes after the noise of them had vanished down the road.

"Do many people go stag-hunting?" she said.

"Fair number," said Mr. Hancock. "And there's them as goes to watch. There's those as doesn't care for it much, too."

"Do you?" said Lucy, "care for it?"

"If it's what you've been born and brought up with you don't think too much about it."

Inside the forge, the cart-horse shifted, and neighed. The smith, reminded of the job in hand, turned and went into the darkness again. Lucy stayed in the lane, scowling to herself.

Caroline and Louise came hurrying past, pink and excited. "Oh, hello, Lucy. I say, did you see the hounds? Mummy said she hoped so because it would be rather a thrill for you."

"Did she?"

"I say, she says Lou and I might be able to hunt this winter! Wouldn't it be marvellous!"

"Would it?" said Lucy. "Why?"

"Yes, of course. Well, I mean, obviously. Why are you staring at me like that, Lucy? I say, let's go and watch them go through the village. They've gone down to the stream that way."

"But that's the way they came," said Lucy, "I saw the marks they made earlier when I was down there with Aunt Mabel."

"Oh no, Lucy. They came straight from the kennels, up the road. They've not been through the village before."

Lucy said slowly, "Are you quite sure? Absolutely sure?"

"Yes, quite sure. Come on, Lou."

Lucy sat on the stone wall by the stream, in the warmth and brightness of the morning. The wall was hot to the touch, the cool water slid below; on the other side the cottage flowers were bright discs of yellow, orange, purple. She felt clammy, her hands sweating and hair clinging damply to her neck.

What were those marks, then, if the hounds didn't come that way . . . ?

* * *

Back at the cottage, Aunt Mabel was working peaceably in the kitchen, arranging plants in jam-jars, printing their names on pieces of paper.

"Oh, there you are. We lost each other somehow. Dear me, you look washed out. I hope you're not sickening for something, Lucy. I'm no good as a nurse."

Lucy sat down at the kitchen table. Her hands, nail-bitten, grubby, and stained with blackberry juice, rested in front of her and she looked at them with detached interest, as though they were someone else's."

"I'm all right. It's just that it's so hot. I wish it would rain."

"I know. We're all waiting for it."

"I tingle inside, as though my bones had electricity in them."

"Dear me, that must be an odd sensation. Perhaps you need exercise. Why not go with Kester for one of those bike-rides you used to do?"

Lucy said nothing. Presently she got up and went to her room.

Sitting at the table, staring out at the heat-soaked hillside beyond, where trees hung motionless over pools of shade as clear-cut as circles of black felt, she wrote to her father:

... We are all waiting for it to rain, only sometimes I am afraid it is not just that we are waiting for. It gets hotter and hotter. Kester and I do not seem to be friends any more. I do not know whose fault it is. I think perhaps it is just something that has happened, and there was nothing we could do about it. Aunt Mabel is very well and sends you her love. It is only three days now till the Fête, and every evening they do this Dance in the field behind the Village Hall. I go to watch, though I do not like it, and so does Kester, but we do not sit together any more.

NINE

"WE'VE GOT TO move all this stuff into the vestry. The Women's Institute want space in the Hall for their exhibition and they say the costumes and everything are cluttering it up. Louise, do stop dropping things—they're getting all dirty."

Caroline was festooned with tights and jerkins, antlers propped over her shoulder like a brace of hockey sticks. Louise trailed behind, laden.

"D'you think you could help, Lucy? We'll have to do at least two more journeys."

They staggered back and forth between the Village Hall and the church. Finally everything was heaped in a mound in the church porch.

"Oh dear, this pair of tights has got torn. We'd better mend it before Mummy sees. She gets so cross about things nowadays."

"Why does she get cross all the time, Caro?"

"I don't know. I expect it's the Fête and everything. She's been working so hard for it."

Lucy, eyeing the antlers stacked against the curve of the

Norman doorway, said, "Where are you supposed to put them?"

"In the vestry. At least that's what the Vicar said. He said better put them there because it's kept locked and there's no risk of anyone getting in and messing about with them."

Caroline heaved the door open and they began to haul the piles of costumes through the cool emptiness of the church.

"Hang on a minute. I'll have to find the key. It's supposed to be kept under the carpet in front of the altar. Yes, here we are."

The vestry was full of dusty sunshine. A wooden table was stacked high with hymn books and a couple of surplices hung from wooden pegs.

"Stand the antlers up in the corner," said Caroline. "We'd better arrange the costumes on these chairs. Put each set together and make sure nothing's missing."

"Where's the Man-woman's skirt?"

"Oh, gosh! Oh, no, it can't have got lost!" There was a frantic search.

"Here it is! I must have dropped it on the path."

"Oh, *Lou! Do* be careful. Mummy'll have a fit if anything else goes wrong. Honestly, you know she said she felt like calling the whole thing off after the Hobby-horse bust the Hobby."

Lucy stopped fiddling with a prayer-book and said sharply, "What did she say?"

"She said if anything else got lost or broken with only a couple of days to go there just wouldn't be time to do anything about it and we'd have to call it off."

"Did she really mean it?"

"Oh, I don't know. It would depend how bad it was, I s'pose."

"But there's all those posters up now," said Louise, "and

the announcements in the paper and everything."

"I know. Anyway, it'll be all right so long as everyone's careful with the things, and no one gets ill or anything. And even if they did there's always the understudies."

"What if it rains?" said Lucy hopefully.

"Oh well, that would be just too bad. Anyway it won't. Honestly, Lucy, you sound as if you wanted it to. It's going to be fun. I'm getting awfully excited. Only two days now."

Lucy stood in the middle of the vestry, staring at the piles of costumes and the branching antlers heaped against the wall.

"Come on, we'd better go back. Wake up, Lucy, I want to lock the door."

The lock clicked shut.

"Here, I'll put the key back for you."

"Oh, thanks awfully, Lucy."

They walked away through the churchyard. Gravestones staggered in the long grass; swallows looped and swerved above them with the precision of stunt pilots.

"We're going to the stables. We hardly seem to get any time for the ponies these days. Do you want to come, Lucy?"

"No, thank you. I've got to go to the shop for Aunt Mabel. 'Bye."

"'Bye."

There were several people in the shop. Lucy stood by the door to wait, watching wasps dodge above a tray of apples.

"Good morning, Mrs. Watts. I seen your things in the produce tent this morning. A lovely display you got."

"I been lucky. My marrows come out just right this year."

"Plums aren't up to much, though."

"That's true. But the flowers should be a good show, with all the sunshine we've had."

Kester's mother came into the shop, and Lucy shrank back among the stacks of tins.

"Morning, Mary. I hear your Kester's been took bad. Nothing much, I hope?"

"Oh, he were poorly yesterday, but he's perking up today, thank you."

"A fever, is it?"

"Not really. It's more like it were something in his mind. He can be a funny lad, sometimes. You can't know what's going on in his head at all."

"Oh, they can give you a lot of worry when they're growing up. Sometimes it's hard to know what to do for the best."

"That's right. Why I remember the time my Mary was a bit of a girl and she..."

The soft voices droned on. Lucy stared at the floor. When her turn came to be served she had quite forgotten what she had come for. Sugar, tea, flour? She gaped, in dumb confusion.

"Never you mind, dear. Have a think while I serve Mrs. Lang."

Lucy recovered herself, and remembered that it was soap powder. As Mrs. Lang turned to go she smiled at her.

"It's ever such a long time since we saw you at the cottage. Been busy with your auntie, have you? Why don't you come back with me and see Kester. He's been like a lost soul this last day or two."

Lucy hesitated. "I don't know..."

"Come along, love. I'm sure he'd be pleased to see you."

"All right."

Her misgivings flowed back as they reached the door of the cottage, Mrs. Lang chattering amiably. She stood in the kitchen, stiff and awkward. "Kester! You've got a visitor, dear . . . Come down a minute."

He came down the stairs slowly.

"Oh, it's you. Hello."

"Hello."

"Why, Kester, you sound that glum . . . Lucy'll be think-ing you're not glad to see her. Don't take no notice of him, love. He's not been himself this last day or two. Look at them circles under his eyes—he looks like he's seen a ghost or summat. Woke up screaming like a baby the night before last, he did. And then wouldn't tell us nothing as to what it were about. Nightmares, I suppose."

"Oh, shut up. Mum. Please."

"Now then, Kester, there's no call to talk like that. I'm taking you to see Dr. Palmer if you don't get some colour in your face soon. Excuse me a minute, dear, while I put the washing out the back."

Alone, they stood staring at each other.

"What's the matter?" said Lucy.

"There's nothing the matter."

"There is. You look peculiar."

"I *am* peculiar."

"Oh, don't be daft. Please tell me."

Picking at the door-frame with his finger-nail, not look-ing at her, he said abruptly, "If you really want to know, I've seen them. That's what."

Lucy said in a whisper, "The Wild Hunt?"

He nodded.

"Oh, Kester . . . Are you sure? P'raps you dreamed it. I hear things at night, and then it's just the leaves and the wind."

He shrugged his shoulders. "Suit yourself."

"You shouldn't have looked. Kester, you shouldn't have done that."

"Why not?"

"Because . . . Because of something your uncle said. No one looks at them. If you do they get some kind of power over you. He said they have to hunt *something*."

"Take no notice and they'll go away, is that it? Like a bad dream."

"Yes," she said eagerly. "Yes, that's it."

"Bad dreams don't always go away that easy. At least mine don't. Anyway, I wanted to."

"You shouldn't. You're mad. Kester, what were they like?"

He looked past her, out of the window. "I couldn't tell you. You wouldn't believe me. You'd have to look yourself. Why don't you?"

"No!"

"I was scared. And at the same time there was part of me that wasn't." He looked directly at her, his eyes enormous: "Lucy, there was part of me that had to look at them."

There was a silence. Then Lucy said, "Was it the night before last?"

"Yes."

"I saw marks down by the stream. Prints of dogs, and horses. Aunt Mabel said the staghounds had been exercising."

"Maybe they had. I don't know. I feel like I don't know anything any more." He looked strained, almost dazed, his eyes circled with shadows like dark bruises.

Mrs. Lang came back into the kitchen.

"Put the kettle on for me, Kester, there's a good boy. Looking forward to the Fête, are you, Lucy? My goodness, it's going to be hot doing the refreshments this year—it gets like an oven in those marquees, with the sun beating down. I forget, are you one of the ones doing this Dance, dear?"

"No," said Lucy.

"I saw them down at the field last night. A bit queer, I thought it were, but they say it'll be ever such a draw. I don't know what put it in the Vicar's head. Mind there's people in the village don't like it a bit—old George Taylor and them. I can't see the harm in it myself, and they say the lads are getting such a lot of fun out of it. Odd, really."

Lucy said nothing, but a warm flush had crept into Kester's thin face, and his eyes sparkled.

"They look a right lot of charlies," he said.

"You wouldn't have thought Jim Thacker and them would take to a thing like that. Not really. But there's no telling, is there? And with the Vicar and Mrs. Norton-Smith so keen. They put a lot of work into it. I hope it'll go off all right."

"Oh, it'll go off," said Kester. "Maybe not quite how they think."

"What do you mean?"

"Wait and see."

Mrs. Lang had turned to the stove, busy with pans, humming to herself.

"Kester, don't do it. Whatever it is you're going to do," said Lucy.

"And why not?"

"Because it'll make things worse, I know it will!"

"I don't know what you're on about. It's the same as up on the moor that day. Why've you come if you're just going to go on at me?"

"Because I'm the only person who can."

"Well, lay off, see."

For a moment they glared at each other in sulky silence. Then Lucy said, "All right, then, I'm going. Do what you like."

"I will, you can bet your life."

Mrs. Lang shut off a tap and turned round: "What's that, dear?"

Lucy said, "I'm sorry, I've got to go. I've just remembered Aunt Mabel wanted me."

"Oh. Nice to have seen you, love."

She sat on the stone wall by the stream, and the village flaunted its preparations at her. Strings of bunting swung above the road, from the recreation ground came the sound of hammering. Mrs. Norton-Smith came bustling past, a sheaf of programmes in her hand, a lorry delivered crates of soft drinks to the Village Hall. And beyond the bright, busy street and the jumbled houses, the woods reached darkly up to the hills, where a line of clouds were gathered in fantastic shapes that made her stare, her fingers digging into the rough edge of the stone.

Later, she went to see Caroline and Louise.

"Are you rehearsing the Dance tonight?"

"Yes. Last time, though. Mummy thinks everyone ought to have a day off tomorrow so's to come fresh to it on the day. Anyway there's tons of other things we've got to do tomorrow. Mummy's going to be busy down at the marquees, and the Vicar's got to organize the Scouts and Guides and all that."

"When?"

"Oh, in the morning, I think. Why do you want to know, Lucy?"

"It doesn't matter."

She laid her plans that evening, sitting at the table in her room, the grey ammonite and the piece of alabaster on the sill in front of her, cradled in cotton-wool. It was lucky the harvest had been so early: that straw-stack in the field beyond the church would do nicely. Some place further away would have been better, but then the journey would take far longer, and, alone, the whole business would take her dangerously long as it was.

What if someone sees me?

She shut the thought from her mind.

Lucy was down at the recreation ground soon after breakfast, lurking in the gateway. She watched Caroline and Louise arrive, trotting in their mother's wake. All three disappeared in the flower tent and Mrs. Norton-Smith's voice, ringing hollowly against the canvas, could be heard bellowing instructions. Presently the Vicar appeared, amid a crowd of Scouts and Guides, and went off to the far corner of the field, where his tall grey figure could be seen dashing hither and thither with chairs, music-stands and long white tapes. Lucy watched for fifteen minutes, and then left.

The church slept peacefully in the sunshine, its squat little tower pink-tinted against the green hillside. There was no sound except for the rooks creaking overhead in the clear sky, and sheep calling in the field beyond, but nevertheless she stood for several minutes outside the porch before plucking up courage to go in.

The key was where she had put it, under the carpet in front of the altar. The noise it made in the lock was startlingly loud, and she glanced uneasily over her shoulder before slipping into the vestry and closing the door behind her.

She had to climb on a chair to open the high window, and then the catch jammed so that she had to struggle for fully a minute before she could get it open. Then she got down again and began to gather up the antlers. They clattered woodenly against each other as she dropped the first half-dozen out of the window and on to the grass below.

Peering out to see where they had fallen, she saw the leather masks staring up at her, the empty eye sockets glowing green. She climbed down again to get the next lot, and flung them after the others. Then she closed the window, put the chair back by the table, and left the vestry, closing the door behind her and returning the key to its hiding-place.

Outside the church, she looked carefully round again. Her mouth was quite dry, and her heart thumped as though it would burst from her chest. Distantly, she could hear the noise from the recreation ground. She went hastily round the back of the church and gathered up an armful of antlers from under the window. She could just carry six at a time, with difficulty. Two journeys would be enough.

There was a convenient hole in the hedge that separated the churchyard from the field. She struggled through it, tearing her bare arms on thorns and catching the antlers in the bushes so that she had to stop and disentangle them. At last she was out the other side. She hesitated, torn for a moment between a quick dash across the middle of the field, and the longer, but more sheltered, route round the edge to the straw-stack in the far corner. She decided on the hedge route, and stumbled round as quickly as she could, half-carrying and half-dragging the antlers.

She pulled them on to the top of the stack, slipping and sliding on the dry straw, coughing as dust flew up and filled her nose and mouth. Scrabbling with her bare hands, pulling bales aside, she made a hollow in the centre, pushed the antlers into it, and shoved the bales on top. Then she slid down the stack and set off back to the churchyard. It had taken over five minutes and she was nearly exhausted.

With the rest of the antlers gathered awkwardly under her arm, she began to cross the churchyard again, a dogged figure ploughing through the thick grass, sweat trickling down her face and wisps of straw clinging to her hair.

"Here! What on earth d'you think you're doing? Put those down at once!"

Lucy whirled round, dropping the antlers. The Vicar was standing against the church wall, anger and astonishment on his face.

He walked across to her. "You're Miss Clough's niece, aren't you?"

Lucy nodded, speechless. The church, the tombstones, the Vicar, spun dizzily for a moment, and then righted themselves. She took a deep breath. No good, all for nothing, might as well give up.

"The rest are in the straw-stack. I'll bring them back." She turned.

"Here, wait a minute." The Vicar took out a large handkerchief and wiped his face. "What were you doing? You'd absolutely no business . . . In any case how did you get into the vestry? Oh, never mind. But *why?*"

"It doesn't matter," said Lucy, "I never really thought it would work, I s'pose." She stood, looking stonily at the ground.

"My dear child," said the Vicar, "I think you really ought to tell me about it. I mean, one's here to help, after all. If you've got some sort of problem perhaps you'd like to talk it over. I mean, there must be some *reason* for this kind of behaviour. Shall we sit down?"

They sat side by side on the grass, Lucy stiff-backed and silent. "You were hiding them in the straw-stack? But, my dear, think what would have happened if we hadn't found them. Why, we might have had to call off the Dance."

Lucy mumbled something.

"What did you say?"

"I said, that's what I wanted."

The Vicar peered at her in perplexity, then, with a sudden

burst of enlightenment he said, "Was it that you were jealous because you weren't taking part? Yes, of course. My dear child, you should have said—I daresay we could have fixed something if you felt so strongly about it."

"Oh, *no*," said Lucy irritably, "of course not."

"We all have unworthy feelings from time to time. You mustn't be ashamed. Perhaps we could still..."

"I didn't *want* to be in it. I think it's daft."

The Vicar said stiffly, "Then that makes your behaviour inexcusable. It's an interesting revival of a very ancient custom, and we hope it's going to make quite a bit of money for the Restoration Fund."

"You don't know anything about it. You don't know what it's going to do. That's just the point."

The Vicar got up. "We really aren't getting anywhere. I'm sorry, I hoped I could help you."

"Are you going to tell everybody?"

"Not necessarily, it wouldn't serve any purpose, so long as you help put them all back. But I feel I must see your aunt—that is one's duty, after all. Tell me," he added delicately, looking at Lucy with a mixture of concern and dislike, "have you been having any—er—family problems?"

She stared over the gravestones, her face burning. Alfred Watts, she read, had died on 23 April 1884, followed by his beloved wife Margaret on 19 February 1890. Next door to them Mary Eliza Tomms rested in peace.

"Sometimes it helps to, er, unburden oneself."

Lucy got up. "I'll bring those things back," she said.

Aunt Mabel was reading the newspaper, Whitby at her feet, twitching in his sleep. Lucy said, in a leaden voice, "I'm sorry, but the Vicar's coming to see you."

"Oh, well, that's not a major disaster. What is it? Recruits for the choir, or a donation to the Restoration Fund?"

"It's about me."

"You?"

"Something I've done. I'm sorry. At least I'm sorry about him coming to see you."

She sat in her room while the voices murmured in the room below. Sometimes the flow shaped itself into words— ". . . adolescent problems . . . behaviour can be difficult to interpret . . . expert guidance sometimes useful"—and then finally Aunt Mabel's voice, crisp and final ". . . most kind of you to call, Vicar . . . really mustn't keep you any longer at this busy time."

The front door slammed.

Later, Aunt Mabel brought up mugs of coffee and sat on the bed. "Not an intelligent man. But well-meaning, I don't doubt."

Lucy peered through her hair, wary.

"Mind, he was justifiably annoyed. What exactly *were* you up to?"

"I wanted to stop them doing this Dance thing."

Aunt Mabel sipped her coffee thoughtfully. "I don't really think you can do that, you know, my dear."

"Yes, I know now. But I had to try, you see."

Aunt Mabel occupied herself with stirring her coffee. Then she said, "It's a pity you and Kester aren't seeing so much of each other. I thought you were getting on so well. But I'm sure it will work out in the end, you know, my dear."

"I expect so," said Lucy dully.

There was a silence. Aunt Mabel pretended to be studying the titles of the books on the shelf. Lucy stared at the floor, her fingers clenched round the handle of her cup. After a few moments she said, "It's not just Kester."

"I know," said Aunt Mabel. "I'm afraid I've not been very much help. It's so difficult to remember—" she hesitated.

Lucy raised her head a little. "Remember what?"

"Remember how one felt at your age. But I do know one was a prey to every kind of uncomfortable imagining. Dreadfully susceptible."

Lucy looked away again. She said stiffly, "I don't know about imagining. It's only real things I get upset about."

Aunt Mabel began to talk in a rush, looking sternly out of the window as though what she was saying was uncomfortable to her. "The point is, you see, that you are so fearfully raw and exposed, you poor dears. Every cold wind blows so very chill. Things become distorted, magnified, even quite transformed. You will find, as you get older, that one grows a kind of protective skin. Things are never quite so bad again: feelings, I mean." She turned to face Lucy, embarrassed, her face a little pink, her nose very shiny, hands smoothing her skirt.

Lucy said, "Oh, I see." Then, because she felt this a poor response, she added, "Good. About the skin, I mean."

"So there you are," said Aunt Mabel, with a return to her old briskness. She got up and went to the door. "And now you really must get an early night. It'll be a full day tomorrow. Good-night, dear."

"Good-night, Aunt Mabel. Oh, and Aunt Mabel..."

"Yes?"

"Thank you."

There was a full moon that night. Lucy lay awake, watching the forked shadows of branches move against the window.

TEN

SHE SAW WHAT had happened as soon as she came down the stairs in the morning. Antlers on three walls, a light patch on the wallpaper, antler-shaped, where the fourth pair had been.

"Aunt Mabel! The antlers have gone again! Really gone. Now I know it's true."

Aunt Mabel appeared at the kitchen door. Whitby came clicking after her and stood, growling fussily.

"How very odd! So they have. Be quiet, dog, it's no good telling us about it now. But how could anyone have taken them without us hearing?"

"It's happened before," said Lucy, "only before they came back."

"Perhaps someone borrowed them for this Dance. Mrs. Norton-Smith, maybe. Odd not to ask, though."

"Ring her up and see. Please, Aunt Mabel, please do."

Three minutes later Aunt Mabel put the receiver down. "She says she doesn't know anything about it. I felt a little foolish, I must admit. But I don't propose to worry—there'll turn out to be a simple explanation. Anyway, I'm not sure

I care for the things all that much. Don't take it to heart so, child."

After breakfast they set off for the recreation ground. Lucy was glad to have been drafted into helping arrange the wild flower exhibition. At least it would fill the morning. The hours ahead, until four o'clock when the Dance was to take place, stretched in front like a series of obstacles. Lucy both wanted to get them behind her, and at the same time dreaded their passage. The time beyond, when it would all be over, the evening, tomorrow, was as unimaginable as next year, or being grown-up. Resigned, almost passive, she followed Aunt Mabel out of the cottage. She was grateful to her: where anyone else would have been murmuring about dresses and clean shoes, her aunt had ignored her jeans and tangled hair. No doubt she had not even seen them.

Outside the shop they met the Norton-Smiths. Lucy had to steel herself to look towards them, but Mrs. Norton-Smith hailed them with her usual jauntiness. Clearly the Vicar had not spoken.

"Hello there! Marvellous day again. Aren't we lucky!"

A woman standing at her gate said, "It'll rain afore night. Look at the colour o' they hills."

They all looked. The hills were mackerel-blue, darkly intense under a cloudless sky.

"They seem the same as they always do to me," said Mrs. Norton-Smith. "I hope you're wrong, anyway."

Down at the recreation ground the loudspeakers croaked fitfully, blaring short bursts of music and then lapsing into silence.

"Where's the electrician? Tell him this thing's gone wrong again."

"Coming, Vicar. Be with you right away."

The strings of bunting sagged in the breathless morning.

Inside the tents it was steamy, like a greenhouse. Lucy arranged flowers in jars, labelled berries and fungi, glanced furtively around.

"We're running out of jars, dear. Go and see if you can borrow some."

She wandered out into the field. There were people everywhere, some purposeful, involved, others merely drifting and offering advice.

"It'll never do, putting the band just there, Vicar, right up against the refreshments. We'll not hear ourselves think."

"That's a point, now. What about the far corner there? But then they're right by the Dog Show?"

Lucy switched direction hastily, and went into the produce tent. "Please, have you any spare jars my aunt could have?"

"Oh, hello, my dear. Yes, I think I've one or two."

Lucy looked round, past kaleidoscopic piles of vegetables, beetroot, carrots, pyramids of marrows. "Is—is Kester here, Mrs. Lang?"

"He come down when I did, but I've not laid eyes on him this last hour or so. Shall I tell him you were looking out for him?"

"No, no thank you. It's all right."

Out in the field, the sun beat down. Wasps danced above the rubbish bins, already the grass was speckled with cigarette packets, lolly sticks, the glitter of silver foil. In the corner, behind the "Dog Show" notice, dogs snapped and howled. Lucy looked across and saw Sheba, crouched nervously against the hedge. On an impulse, she went across and stared closely at the animal: the eyes were quite brown, there was no doubt of that. But suddenly it swung its head in alarm, and there was a green glint. She frowned, and turned away.

"Hello, Lucy. Did your aunt find her antlers? Mummy

was awfully sorry she couldn't help but she really hadn't a clue about them."

"No. No, she didn't."

"Oh well, I 'spect they'll turn up. Isn't it boiling? Honestly, we'll just *die* doing the Dance."

The morning wore on. Aunt Mabel completed her arrangement, and went home.

"Do you want to come with me, or stay?"

"I think I'll stay."

"Just as you like. Come back later for something to eat before the festivities begin."

Once she saw Kester, standing idly against the wall, staring out across the field. He took a step towards her and she thought he was going to speak, but he walked away over the grass, whistling.

At midday she returned to the cottage. The tarmac was sticky in the heat, though the sun was blotted out, not so much by cloud as a thickening of the very air, so that the sky seemed to press down on the valley. Lucy's head ached.

When she returned to the recreation ground an hour or so later the village was throbbing with activity—people leaving their houses, cars driving into the field beyond the church that had been made into a car park. It was still heavy and sultry, the flags hanging limp above the street. At the field, the loudspeakers quacked instructions, the Vicar's voice sounding bizarrely distorted. The car park was rapidly filling up and strange faces mingled now with the villagers, people in holiday clothes and with different accents, towing small children, wandering here and there among the marquees.

The Vicar strode over the grass, rubbing his hands and beaming, "Good crowd, eh? We look like doing well. Anyone seen Mrs. Norton-Smith?"

Lucy hunted for Kester, and could not find him.

"What *are* you doing, Lucy? You've walked right round the field three times now. Lou and I were watching."

"Nothing, really."

"Don't you want to see the opening? Come and stand here with us."

"What opening?"

"Opening the Fête, silly."

A big car, very clean, very black, drew up in front of the Village Hall and was met by an obsequious group composed of the Vicar and other members of the committee. A woman in a large hat emerged from it and drifted over the grass with the Vicar towards the trestle table and chairs ranged under the big oak tree.

"That's Lady Somebody," said Caroline, awed.

"What's she for?"

"To open it, of course."

"Why her, specially? Because she's Lady Somebody?"

"I 'spose so," said Caroline. "I mean, it makes her more interesting to look at, doesn't it?"

"No," said Lucy, staring.

The Lady was presented with a bunch of flowers, murmured something into the microphone, and the Fête was opened. People began to stream in and out of the marquees; in the far corner the band struck up, the Guides were demonstrating first aid in another corner, the Dog Show was getting under way, the loudspeakers crackled announcements.

Caroline said, "We'd better go and change now. It's only about half an hour till the Dance."

Alone, Lucy wandered to and fro. She felt detached, as though she existed in a private vacuum, quite insulated from the people around her. They interested her in no way at all, their faces passed and re-passed her like a series of masks, their chattering voices barely audible. She was stiff with anticipation.

A hand was laid on her arm. The smith said, "You seen young Kester this afternoon?" There was a trace of urgency in his voice, a flicker in his eyes that might have been anxiety.

"No," said Lucy. "I've looked all over. D'you think he's stayed away?"

"I do not. He'd not do that."

The Vicar's distorted voice blared across the field, "Ladies and Gentlemen, please . . . The chief item in our programme this afternoon is the performance of the Horn Dance of Hagworthy, a revival of an ancient festivity which we understand was carried on in these parts in former times. The Dancers will perform the opening section of the Dance here in the recreation ground, and then progress through the village and round the valley according to the old ritual. Would you please clear a space in the centre of the field for them."

"Interferin' fool," said the smith suddenly, still with his hand on Lucy's arm. "What do he think he's about? I tell you he don't know what he's doing."

Lucy stared at him. People eddied round them: fragments of conversation, bursts of laughter, children shouting.

"What—what might he have done?"

"Eh?"

She said in a rush, "I must know, Mr. Hancock. Please. What is it about the Dance? There's something, isn't there? I've always felt there was."

"It weren't never a Dance. Maybe it were a Dance in other parts, but it weren't a Dance here. Least not a Dance like he's got in mind. There were more to it than dancing."

The loudspeaker was playing records: a continuous stream

of cheerful, bouncy have-a-good-time music.

"If it's not a Dance, what is it, then, Mr. Hancock?"

The man replied, staring over the bright faces towards the Village Hall. "It were a Hunt, girl, that's what. It were a Stag Hunt. And there were always one as had to run as the Stag. And it weren't no game, either."

Lucy breathed deeply. "I see. Yes, I thought it must be something like that."

The Dancers were emerging from the Village Hall, a straggling, self-conscious group in their absurd costumes. People stared and chattered.

"It were best forgot," said the smith savagely. "No good ever come of it."

"Who—who had to be the Stag? In the old days?"

"It were the one as the other lads had took against. Anyone as set theirselves apart from the rest, like."

Cold hands seemed to clutch at Lucy. She said, "What happened to them?"

"He'd get a ducking, most likely. But sometimes it were worse. That's why they put a stop to it."

"What's it got to do with—with the other Hunt?" said Lucy, in a whisper.

"It growed out of it, didn't it? There was always folk remembered it, and those as still saw it, and there were the stags up on the hill to make us think of it. This has always been hunting country, round here."

Lucy stood quite still, jostled by people moving around her, gazing at the flaring antlers above the masks. She felt mesmerized, unable to do anything but stand and watch. Images flickered before her eyes, not of the shifting crowd or the spreading shapes of the marquees, but of Kester's face above the stream, dappled with reflected light: the neat spirals of ammonites: the dark outline of a dog in the night: the frozen movement of the picture on the stairs.

Mr. Hancock was saying something. Lucy jumped, and the images dissolved. "I'm sorry?"

"I said as I'm off now. I'm not stopping for any more o' this nonsense." There was a muscle twitching in his cheek, and his glance roved over the field, searching uneasily.

"If you see Kester, tell him I were looking for him."

Lucy, watching the Dancers fan out over the grass, said, "He'll be all right, won't he? Even if—if it was a Hunt again?"

"There's no saying, is there, girl? And there's the other, too. The dancing always brought them back."

"He says he's seen them already. The other night."

The man turned on her sharply, "He said that? He's a fool, then. We don't look at them. Not nowadays." He dug his hands into his pockets, scowling over the heads around them. After a moment he said, "Do you want to help him, then?"

"What?"

"I said as you could help him, if that's what you want." He was reaching in his pocket for something. "If there's trouble, and there has to be, now it's gone this far, give him this. He should hold it in his hand."

It was a horse-shoe. The rusty iron was cold to the touch, and rough. Lucy took it from him, glancing at it for a moment.

"This?"

"Aye, that," he said irritably. "Don't act stupid, girl. Just do as I'm telling you. Cold iron always had the power to send 'em back where they came from. They come from old times, see, and we use the old things against them. And don't look at them, girl. Nor him neither. Tell him that."

He moved off and began to shoulder his way through the crowd, leaving her alone in a mass of strange faces and voices. She thrust the lump of iron in her pocket and stared again at the Dancers. She could see them start to prance and leap: the music whined across the grass as the loud-speaker crackled into silence. People strained forward to get a better view and there were murmurs here and there.

"Isn't it peculiar! They do look a bit funny, don't they?"

"Mummy! What's the people jumping up and down for? Why've they got those things on their faces?"

The Dancers leaped and turned, forming arches, winding back into a chain, circling each other. The Fool's bells jangled in the still air, the antlers, touching one another, clicked and thumped, the Dancers' feet brushed the dry grass. The sky above them was no longer blue but a soupy dun-colour, and distantly beyond the hills, thunder rolled. The Vicar, standing at the table, the microphone in his hand, glanced upwards uneasily. The Dancers uncurled into a sin-gle line and filed off towards the road, still leaping and jigging, the crowd parting to make way for them. The pace seemed to have quickened, and the music to have taken on a note of frenzy. The Hobby-horse kept darting into the crowd, shaking the Hobby and grabbing at people. There was laughter, and less approving comments.

"Here, you keep off! That's not funny."

"Mind what you're doing, will you! Get away . . ."

Mrs. Norton-Smith left her place at the table and hurried after the Dancers, looking flushed.

The antlers only could be seen now, bobbing above the heads of the crowd. The Hobby-horse, momentarily sepa-rated from the others, was chasing some shrieking girls near the gate. Lucy looked towards the line of Dancers, slowed up now by the crowd. Surely . . .? She began to push through the crowd to get nearer, panting a little.

There were still people coming into the recreation ground through the gate, and others making their way towards the road to watch the Dancers leave. The converging streams met, trapping the Dancers between them: the antlers swayed above the heads. The Vicar's voice boomed over the field, with a note of desperation—"Please clear a path for the Dancers to leave the field. Stand aside please, down by the gate . . ."

The Hobby-horse had rejoined the others. Lucy, with a last frantic shove, reached a clear patch of high ground by the hedge and stared across at them. Yes, it was as she had thought: where there should be twelve Dancers there were now thirteen.

And as she looked something seemed to be happening in the midst of the group of Dancers. Antlers clashed, no longer accidentally, there were shouts of, "Steady on, there!" "Here, stop that!" People began backing hastily away, isolating the Dancers, and then suddenly one of the figures broke away and began running for the entrance, followed by several others, no longer making any pretense at dancing but pushing and shoving anyone in their path, brandishing the antlers like weapons, shouting to one another. The Vicar dropped the microphone and started to run over the grass.

"What a shambles!" said a disgusted voice. "Really, I must say!"

The girl Dancers were left standing disconsolately by the gate. Caroline dropped her mask and antlers and began to cry, the tears glistening on her sweat-streaked face.

The crowd broke up. People wandered away towards the tents, laughing and talking. Some were indignant.

"Really, one comes all this way to see this thing and then the organizers let them get quite out of hand!"

"Weren't it funny, Mum, when they all begun fighting!"

"I didn't quite understand, dear, were they supposed to do that or not? All chasing that boy?"

Lucy ran towards the gate and stared up the lane. The

bright figures of the Dancers were some way away now, running wildly through the village and up the valley. She saw Jim Thacker's tawny head, and the branching antlers propped over his shoulder as he ran. They were running fast, purposefully. She could not see Kester.

The Vicar was standing near, occasionally taking a few steps up the road after the vanishing Dancers, then returning to look anxiously round. "Really, I am deeply annoyed about this. I shall have a lot to say to those boys—it's absolutely disgraceful behaviour. We've been completely let down. Oh, there you are, Mrs. Norton-Smith. This is quite deplorable, isn't it?"

There was the shrill pitch of hysteria in Mrs. Norton-Smith's voice. "I always thought something like this would happen. You never took a tough enough line with those boys, Vicar, if I may say so."

"Well, really, one was doing one's best. And with my experience of Youth work..."

"Actually the whole thing was a pretty odd idea. I always had my doubts."

"But I understood you to be so keen..."

"And with the way people have been going on about it in the village, one really wonders if there isn't something in it... You should have given the whole thing up."

"Mummy..." said Caroline imploringly, "don't go on."

"Well, I *must* say!" snapped the Vicar. "One doesn't expect such disloyalty." They stood glaring at one another.

"Why did Kester join in suddenly?" said Louise.

"Kester Lang? Don't be silly, dear, he wasn't one of them."

"Yes, he was. He was there all of a sudden, with antlers and everything."

"Rubbish. Come along, girls, we're going home. I have the most appalling headache."

Lucy said wildly, "It's your fault—all of you. You started it all up again—and now Kester has to be the Stag. They knew it from the beginning, he and the other boys—and none of them could stop it once it was begun. If anything happens to Kester it'll be your fault." She was almost shouting.

Mrs. Norton-Smith said, "Somebody should do something about that girl. I don't want to be uncharitable but I really don't think she's normal." She turned back into the field, her face blotchy with passion.

Lucy pushed up towards the hills. The Dancers had vanished, but one or two people were still staring after them. An old woman said, "It were bound to turn out like that, weren't it? Will they catch 'e?"

"I 'ope not."

When she reached the twist in the road beyond the pub she had a clear view of the big field stretching up beyond the stream. There were seven brightly coloured figures strung out over the stubble, the leading one ahead by only a few yards. Some of them had discarded most of their costumes: the Man-woman's skirt was flung over a hedge and the Fool's cap and bells lay down by the stream. Jim Thacker's ginger hair and thick-set body were identifiable even at this distance. As Lucy splashed through the stream and began to climb the hill after them drops of rain were falling, as thick and warm as the air itself, trickling down her face and making the grass slippery under her feet.

The last of the Dancers had plunged over the bank at the top before she was half-way up the field. Beyond lay the first bracken-covered reach of the moor, and as she climbed the bank she could see their heads above the green, nearer now, forging ahead like swimmers, quite silent. She could pick out Kester, still not far ahead of his pursuers, and as she paused, gasping to get her breath back, he hesitated for a moment, looking around, and the gap closed a little.

He had to make a choice: straight on up the rise of the hill towards the open moor, or down the steep, wooded plunge into the next combe to Hagworthy, called Sweetwater because of the big stream that flowed down it from Exmoor. He paused just for an instant, and must have decided on the second, for he swung to the right and began to descend the hill.

"No!" shouted Lucy, "don't go down to the water!" but her voice sounded faint and weak, blotted out at once in the heavy air. The Dancers did not even turn their heads, changing direction to follow Kester. They disappeared among the trees, and birds lifted from the branches as they did so, disturbed—a heron, flapping away up the combe, jackdaws, a buzzard circling effortlessly upwards. Lucy stumbled through the last few yards of bracken and over a low wall in amongst the trees.

It was very steep, the hillside pitching down into the narrow combe, and far below she could hear the rush of the water, muted by the thick growth of oak and beech, but still loud above the softer rustlings and murmurings of the undergrowth. It was dry under the trees, though the rain tapped the leaves overhead and somewhere far away thunder growled over the moor. She could no longer see the Dancers, but crashings and the sway of branches betrayed their presence further down the combe.

Where would Kester go? The combe was one of the places Lucy had visited with him earlier in the summer, riding their bikes down the rough track beside the stream and then abandoning them as the water narrowed near the top to climb the steep sides that she was now descending. Further down the water was wide, running swift over the stones towards the old pack-horse bridge at the bottom; up here, in the neck of the combe, it was narrow and deep, bridged only in one place by a plank. That, surely, would be where Kester planned to cross the stream and perhaps, like the stags themselves, throw off his pursuers. She plunged down through the trees, sliding on the moss below, with the roar of the water getting louder all the time. She could hear the Dancers shouting to each other.

"Where's 'e gone? I can't see 'im no more."

"This way—over here! He be making for the water."

Suddenly the water, and the plank, came into sight below her, and Kester too, scrambling down towards the stream. Before she could stop herself she had called his name, and his face, white and startled, turned and looked back at her, and he paused, one foot on the plank. And the hunters too had heard, casting about the banks of the water further down, for they shouted to one another and came weaving back through the trees. Lucy saw their faces, strangely distorted, bestial in this chase that was no longer a game between boys.

She shouted, "Go on, Kester, go on. Don't stop!"

He crossed the plank, hesitated only a moment and then vanished into the trees on the far side. The Dancers were still ranging up and down, converging now on the plank. Lucy reached it before the first of them and ran across, her feet sliding horribly on the damp surface. Then she scrabbled in the mossy bank for the end of it and with a massive effort prised it up and flung it away from her into the stream. It tipped into the water with a splash, and Jim Thacker pulled himself up short on the other side, heaving and panting, red-faced, his eyes glazed.

Lucy shouted, "Stop! Just stop it, all of you! Have you gone mad or something?"

The sweat was pouring off his forehead and he put up a

hand to wipe it away, staring at her confusedly. The other boys were calling to him, "Go on, Jim. Get after him! Never mind the water."

Lucy said again, "Stop it! What do you think you're doing? It's over now. The Dance is over."

One of them made a movement towards her and then pulled back uncertainly, shaking his head like a dog. They all had a dazed, stupefied look about them.

Jim Thacker said, "It's that girl again. What's she doin' here?" He seemed to subside, the fury gone from him, staring round in bewilderment. "We was after Kester Lang, wasn't we? I reckon we gone a bit too far."

"It were that old Dance. It got into us, like."

They were looking from one to another uneasily, and then across at Lucy, making the slow journey back to reality, becoming once again a group of ordinary boys. Lucy, still crouched beside the stream, watching them, felt the fear ebb from her and thought: it was seeing me like that when they weren't expecting it, and me shouting at them—it kind of put them back into their minds again. Strangely, she felt sorry for them, touched by their confusion. One of them said angrily, "It were a fool idea o' theirs, anyways, that Dance."

"Let's be getting back, then."

"Come on. Who cares about Kester Lang? Let 'im be." The Fool flung his antlers into the water irritably. The rest turned and began to move away up the hillside, whistling and calling to one another.

Lucy watched them go. As their voices faded away the combe became very still, only the water ran steadily below her and the rain pattered on the leaves. It was dark too, with no sunlight filtering down from above, a deep green twilight in which only the spread shapes of the branches moved. She stayed for several minutes, staring across at the other side of the combe, until the boys disappeared over the lip of the hill. The private sounds of the place began again, wood-pigeons rumbling, the shriek of a jay, inexplicable scurryings and rushings that ceased as suddenly as they began. Then she got up and began to climb upwards, between the slanting trunks of the trees, calling, "Kester! Kester, it's all right now!" But there was no reply, and when she stopped to listen there was nothing but the falling rain, the water below and the swaying branches.

When she reached the top her throat was dry with effort, and her hands sore where she had grabbed at branches and stumps to pull herself up. The hillside stretched open before her, coarse grass with scatterings of bracken and heather and here and there a blaze of gorse. Black-faced sheep turned to stare, and then moved on. Lucy stood for a moment, looking all around, down into the deep cleft of Sweetwater, running green and dense into the vale, to the heather-covered brow of the hill above Hagworthy, and ahead to the open moor, reaching away under a clouded sky to the sea. There was no living thing in sight but the sheep, tiny birds flitting from one hillock of grass to another, and the buzzard floating above. It mewed, a sad, plaintive sound, and somewhere in the combe a raven croaked.

She began to climb higher up the hill, heading for the tumbledown stone wall at the top. Against the skyline the clouds were dark, shifting shapes rimmed with light from an unseen sun: they moved swiftly, forming and re-forming, dissolving into one another, racing against the wide sweep of the sky above the silent hillside. Lucy was seized with a sudden panic and began to run, calling Kester's name again. The rain ran down her face and a chill little wind licked at her arms and pulled back her damp hair.

She scrambled over the wall, and another bleak stretch of the moor confronted her. But now, in the middle distance, there was a figure running through the heather, stumbling, picking itself up again, running with a terrible urgency.

She shouted, "Kester! It's me! It's over, they've gone. There's only us here."

He turned sharply and looked back at her, and as he did so it seemed to Lucy that she could hear a noise, a pattering louder than the hiss of the rain on the bracken. It came from all around, and from the sky above, and as Kester turned his head from side to side, searching the moor, she knew he could hear it too. She hesitated, and black shapes swept around her, dark shadows streaming over the heather. Reflections of the clouds, running on the ground below? She looked up, but the sky was dark, no longer shot with light from a hidden sun and in that moment she knew that there were no shadows.

Kester was crouched in the bracken, transfixed like a hunted animal, and beyond him there were dark things leaping and bounding through the heather, and for the instant that Lucy allowed herself to look at them she saw the flash of a green that was not grass, an emerald fire from eyes and mouths, and in the far distance something else came moving effortlessly down the hill, flowing dark and silent over the ground, a shape that was crowned with a great spread of antlers. And Kester, too, was slowly rising, and turning to look behind him.

She shrieked, "Don't look! Kester, don't look!" and rushed towards him, her eyes down so that she could no longer see them but only hear that insistent noise, the gathering thunder above the wind and the rain. She was aware of movement all around, the moor itself seemed to surge and run with her, closing in on the still figure of Kester.

There was something hard digging into her thigh. She thrust her hand in her pocket and felt the horseshoe, quite forgotten until that moment. She tugged it out as she ran, and clutched it tight. The shapes were behind Kester now, and coming from all sides, whipping through the bracken like darkness itself. Lucy, looking fully at him as she raced the last few yards, held out the cold iron and he put out his hand as though in a trance and his fingers closed around it. They were holding it together as they rolled down into the bracken and as they did so the air was rushing all around them and the pattering and snuffling loud in their ears. She felt Kester's hand warm against hers, clenched on the metal, and they both pressed their faces down into the damp heather. For moments they crouched there, fighting the instinct to get up and run, and as they lay the moor subsided about them, the movements seemed to rise like a wind and sweep away above the hillside and beyond towards the sea, and when at last they sat up and looked around there was only the soft curve of the moor and, above, gulls floating white against a grey sky shadowed with the drifting shapes of clouds.

They stared at each other.

"Did you see them?" said Kester. "Did you?"

"I don't know . . . Yes, I think so. I mean, I know I did. But it's all different now." Wind rippled the bracken, but only the white humps of sheep moved against the green. The rain had stopped; down in the vale columns of sunlight poured on to fields and hedges. Lucy pushed tangled hair from her eyes and sat, arms clasped round her knees, frowning slightly.

Kester was still holding the horseshoe, and looking at it as though aware of it for the first time.

"What's this, then?"

"Your uncle gave it to me. He said it would—stop them. That, and not looking. You would *look*, Kester. He was worried about you, your uncle—terribly."

"Was he?" Kester sat still for a moment, staring over the

hillside. He fingered the piece of iron for a moment and then sent it spinning away into the heather and grinned. "He's a funny bloke, Uncle Tom. I say, what happened to Jim Thacker and the others?"

"They stopped at the stream, when they saw me. I shouted at them, and they suddenly went all different—as though they'd, well, woken up or something. They even looked different. Their faces weren't all—you know, like they were before. Kind of mad."

Kester nodded. "I feel like I've just woken up, too." They sat in silence for a few moments, then Lucy said, "It was all rather horrible, really."

"I'll say. I was dead scared, I can tell you that. I felt they might do anything."

"But it was you as much as them, Kester. As though you wanted it to happen."

"I know. But I couldn't help it, I really couldn't. I kept doing things I didn't really want to do. Going on at you like that, for one."

"It's all right," said Lucy. She shifted slightly, and raindrops showered down from the bracken on to her hands and face. They grinned at each other.

"Let's go," said Kester. "I wonder what happened to their old Fête."

They began to run down the side of the combe, plunging noisily through the bracken, jumping over logs, scattering the sheep. At the edge of the trees they stopped, both together, and looked back for a moment at the hillside.

"We did see them, didn't we?" said Lucy in a whisper.

"Yes. Yes, we did."

They stopped by the stream at the bottom, and Kester waded into the water to fish out the end of the plank and notch it back on to the bank. The Hobby-horse was lying against a tree-stump, half in the water. He picked it up and flung it away into the undergrowth before they began the steep scramble up the other side.

They saw Jim Thacker and the others from the far side of the field above the village, scattered along the wall by the stream, skimming stones in the water. When Lucy and Kester came up to them Jim put two fingers in his mouth and let out a screeching whistle.

"Shut up, you," said Kester amiably. Lucy looked away, uneasy, but the boys ignored her completely. She might have been a bush or a tree. She looked at their untroubled faces, sunburned and cheerful, and then at Kester, with his hands thrust in his pockets, scuffing patterns in the dust with his toe as he shouted remarks at them across the water.

"Coming for a swim then, Kester?"

"I dunno. I might."

"Suit yourself."

The boys drifted away to the pool. Lucy and Kester crossed the field and made their way to the village down the lane. Hagworthy had the seedy, run-down appearance of some seaside resort at the end of an August weekend. Tattered paper and cigarette cartons littered the road, the air smelt of petrol fumes; in the recreation ground the marquees were sinking like deflated balloons as workmen pulled at the ropes. But above the tawdry strings of the bunting and the line of cars bumping their way out of the car park the great stretch of the moor against the sky, and the sentinel trees on the skyline above the combe, were as they had always been. A mist was creeping up the valley, sliding above the road and wreathing the dark trees so that they appeared to rise from a still, white sea.

"All right?" said Kester.

Lucy said, "Yes, I'm all right."

"You know, I feel bad about your aunt's antlers. I'll go and see her. I don't even know what I've done with them. I must have dropped them somewhere."

"I don't think she'll mind all that much. She's not all that keen on them."

"I don't know what made me do it: it was like something was pushing me, from the moment I saw them and the moment I first saw the Dance. And I could never explain to anyone. Not even you."

Lucy nodded.

A woman came out of a cottage, looked sharply at Kester, and went in again. Through the open doorway they heard her voice.

"They boys 'as come back, I see."

"I'm glad of that."

"Vicar'll have summat to say. Hopping mad, he were."

"It was a silly idea all along, I reckon."

"Aye, it were."

Lucy stopped outside her aunt's cottage. "I'd better go in. She'll be wondering. We've been gone ages." Indeed, as the mist thickened, dusk had begun to fall, and lights glimmered here and there in the windows. It was cool, with a rich, damp smell drifting from the hedgerows.

"Right," said Kester. "We'll go out on the bikes tomorrow, shall we?"

"Yes. Yes, I'd like that."